"I'd like to know how you can be a virgin and have a baby."

The embers of her passion died, leaving her drained. Why hadn't she stopped him before he found out the truth? The answer was as blinding as the joy he had made her feel. Until he knew everything, she had no chance of a future with him. Against all reason, she yearned for one.

"Joel isn't my baby."

His cold tone sliced to her heart. "Obviously not. So who does he belong to?"

She took a deep breath to subdue the anguish threatening to consume her. "You," she said softly. "You're Joel's father, Sam."

Dear Reader,

As senior editor for the Silhouette Romance line, I'm lucky enough to get first peek at the stories we offer you each month. Each editor searches for stories with an emotional impact, that make us laugh or cry or feel tenderness and hope for a loving future. And we do this with *you,* the reader, in mind. We hope you continue to enjoy the variety each month as we take you from first love to forever....

Susan Meier's wonderful story of a hardworking single mom and the man who sweeps her off her feet is *Cinderella and the CEO.* In *The Boss's Baby Mistake,* Raye Morgan tells of a heroine who accidentally gets inseminated with her new boss's child! The fantasy stays alive with Carol Grace's *Fit for a Sheik* as a wedding planner's new client is more than she bargained for....

Valerie Parv always creates a strong alpha hero. In *Booties and the Beast,* Sam's the strong yet tender man. Julianna Morris's lighthearted yet emotional story *Meeting Megan Again* reunites two people who only *seem* mismatched. And finally Carolyn Greene's *An Eligible Bachelor* has a very special secondary character—along with a delightful hero and heroine!

Next month, look for our newest ROYALLY WED series with Stella Bagwell's *The Expectant Princess.* Marie Ferrarella astounds readers with *Rough Around the Edges*—her 100th title for Silhouette Books! And, of course, there will be more stories throughout the year chosen just for you.

Happy reading!

Mary-Theresa Hussey

Mary-Theresa Hussey
Senior Editor

Please address questions and book requests to:
Silhouette Reader Service
U.S.: 3010 Walden Ave., P.O. Box 1325, Buffalo, NY 14269
Canadian: P.O. Box 609, Fort Erie, Ont. L2A 5X3

Booties and
the Beast

VALERIE PARV

SILHOUETTE *Romance*®

Published by Silhouette Books

America's Publisher of Contemporary Romance

For my sisters Maureen and Leigh, with love

SILHOUETTE BOOKS

ISBN 0-373-19501-X

BOOTIES AND THE BEAST

Copyright © 2001 by Valerie Parv

This edition published by arrangement with Harlequin Books S.A.

Visit Silhouette at www.eHarlequin.com

Printed in U.S.A.

VALERIE PARV

lives and breathes romance and has even written a guide to being romantic, crediting her cartoonist husband of nearly thirty years as her inspiration. As a former buffalo and crocodile hunter in Australia's Northern Territory, he's ready-made hero material, she says.

When not writing her novels and nonfiction books, or speaking about romance on Australian radio and television, Valerie enjoys dollhouses, being a *Star Trek* fan and playing with food (in cooking, that is). Valerie agrees with actor Nichelle Nichols, who said, "The difference between fantasy and fact is that fantasy simply hasn't happened yet."

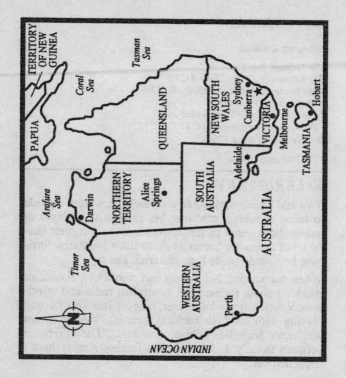

Chapter One

Now that Haley Glen was actually standing at the gates of Sam Winton's mansion she wasn't sure she could go through with her plan. Everything in her wanted to grab him by the throat and not let go until he admitted that he was the father of her sister's baby boy.

Joel was six months old now and Ellen had been gone for five of those months, but this was Haley's first chance to get near the man. She hadn't anticipated being gripped by a wave of last-minute nerves that threatened to paralyze her.

She reminded herself that it had taken all her powers of persuasion to get her friend, Miranda Holt, to send her to this interview. If she chickened out now, she would be letting her friend down as well as Ellen and the baby, so she had no choice but to see it through.

If it killed her.

On a heavy sigh, she reached for the intercom button and took out some of her frustration by punching it savagely and holding it down longer than was polite. From somewhere in the grounds of the mansion, she heard the howl of what sounded like a very large dog.

Moments later an angry voice boomed through the speaker, "No need to ram it through the fence. State your name and business."

She bit back a suggestion of her own about where he could ram the intercom and said as sweetly as she could, "I'm Haley Glen from the HomeBody Agency to see Sam Winton about your house sitter." She was gambling that the voice belonged to Sam himself but something in his tone made her think she was right.

She was. "I'm Winton. What's wrong with Miranda?"

Miranda was the owner of the HomeBody Agency. Normally she would see a client as important as Sam herself and Winton was obviously well aware of it. "She's tied up with…" As her annoyance grew, Haley swallowed the rest of her apology for Miranda's absence. "Do you think we could discuss this face-to-face, Mr. Winton? Or would you rather conduct the entire meeting by intercom?"

A buzz like a swarm of angry bees drowned out his reply as the tall, iron gates swung gracefully inward. Haley got back into her car and drove through. As soon as she had cleared the gates they closed behind her. Common sense told her they were triggered by some kind of sensor mechanism, but she felt an uncomfortable sensation of prison doors clanging shut.

She pulled up outside the imposing Federation-style house and got out but was stopped by a blur of movement she caught out of the corner of her eye. The owner of the Baskerville howl came tearing around the side of the house, churning gravel under its floor mop feet. Haley barely had time to scramble back into the car and pull the door shut, before a dog the size of a small pony threw itself at the window. Her heart pounded as she stared down a throat rimmed by teeth that would have done a shark proud.

"Down, Dougal. Heel."

The command was given with all the authority of a major general, so Haley wasn't surprised when the dog bolted away from her car window as if shot. Had the command been directed at her, she would probably have obeyed it, too. She shivered and wondered if it was from reaction to the sudden appearance of the dog—or its master.

Haley was relieved when the dog settled itself meekly at the heels of the man waiting at the foot of the front steps. It was Sam Winton himself, she saw, recognizing him from the photograph on his books. Except that her first sight of him in the flesh destroyed most of her preconceptions in one go.

She didn't know what she had expected the children's writer to look like, but it wasn't this vibrant man who exuded energy the way high-voltage wires hum with power. His skin was burnished with healthy color, and his hair was as black as baby Joel's only a lot thicker. It curled almost to his collar, it was in a style that reminded her of medieval knights in old movies, though instead of armor this knight was poised in an ivory polo shirt and chinos as black as his hair.

She was used to thinking of him as The Beast, her sister's nickname for him, but he didn't look in the least beastly. He was taller than she had imagined, perhaps half a head taller than Haley herself. He was also well built, but not with the showy musculature of an athlete as much as someone who simply took care of himself.

Right now, the most beastly thing about him was the deep vee of a frown that cut a swathe between two of the bluest eyes she had ever seen. His frown deepened as she looked warily at the dog. "You can get out now. He won't hurt you."

When she did so, the man reached for her hand and a jolt like electricity surged along her arm, affirming the high-voltage impression she'd already formed. She tried to pull away but his grip was like steel. Alarm shrilled through her. "What are you..."

He offered her hand to Dougal, who sniffed it, making her wonder if the dog's next move would be to swallow her hand up to the wrist. He looked more than capable of it. But Sam said, "Friend, Dougal. Friend."

At first the dog's tail moved listlessly then waved like a banner in a stiff breeze and he gave her hand in Sam's a mighty lick. Relief coursed through her and she rubbed the dog's shaggy chest with her free hand. His wiry coat teased her palm and he lowered his great head and butted her gently. She smiled, wondering how she could have been afraid of the shaggy animal for a minute. "Good dog."

Sam nodded approvingly, obviously noting that she hadn't made the elementary mistake of trying to pat the dog on the head. "You know dogs?"

"I love them. When I was a child, I had an Australian kelpie called Buddy." The feel of her hand in his distracted her, making it hard to think straight.

He didn't seem to notice her discomfort, keeping his fingers threaded through hers as he straightened. "You bolted as soon as Dougal appeared."

Naturally, he'd seen her undignified scramble back into the car. It put her at a further disadvantage and she drew herself up defensively. "For all I knew, he was a guard dog, trained to eat intruders." She didn't add, "like his owner," but it must have been in her voice.

When he released her hand, she chased away a surprising sensation of disappointment. "Dougal is supposed to be a guard dog, but he's more likely to lick an intruder to death in his joy at having company."

A feeling not shared by his owner, she thought, not sure where the certainty came from. "Do you get many intruders?"

"Not with Dougal around. Off you go. Finish your bone." At the magic word, the dog's ears twitched and he loped back the way he'd come. Sam gestured toward the steps. "Shall we go inside?"

His sudden switch to a businesslike tone chilled the atmosphere as effectively as a stiff breeze shredding a mist. For a moment she wondered if he could possibly know who she was, then realized that his anger was in response to hers. This would never do if she was to get to know him better. "I'm sorry if I sounded rude down the intercom when I arrived," she said, biting back any hint of self-justification by reminding herself that Miranda trusted her to behave herself.

"You did," he agreed, "But you also had a point."

His response told her it was as close to an apology as she was going to get so she followed him into the rambling old house. He led the way down a wide arched hallway past a double living room furnished with wonderful antique furniture, past the partially open door of a bedroom that looked recently vacated. Had he been sleeping in the middle of the afternoon? she wondered. But then he was a writer. He probably worked unconventional hours.

He pulled the bedroom door shut before she could do more than glimpse a vast four-poster bed covered in rumpled bedclothes that suggested he was either the world's most restless sleeper or did some of his entertaining in bed.

The thought troubled her, making her wonder why it was harder to think of him as a beast, lonely and unloved, than as a sexual athlete for whom her sister had been one of many conquests. Both images took her into territory she resisted exploring. His personal life had nothing to do with her reason for wanting to meet him.

He opened another door on a vast library with floor-to-ceiling shelves crammed with books. Many of them were reference books on a wide variety of subjects, she saw when she scanned them with instinctive curiosity. Off the library, another door led to what looked like an office, judging by the computers, printers and other paraphernalia visible through the opening. His work space looked chaotic. Surprising, she thought, since he appeared to be the kind of man who liked his life run with military precision.

"Take a seat." He gestured to a leather-covered couch. Iron-gray hairs scattered over the soft leather suggested that Dougal often kept him company while he worked. The thought almost made her melt until she resolutely drove it away. So he allowed his dog to sleep on an obviously expensive piece of furniture. So what? It didn't make Sam any less The Beast than before.

"Coffee?" Sam asked as she perched on the edge of the sofa. He probably thought she feared getting dog hair on her clothes. If he knew the real reason why she was so on edge, he'd probably command his dog to see her on her way.

"Thank you," she said. Socializing with Sam Winton wasn't part of her plan, but the liquid might help to ease the dryness in her throat. "I like it black with no sugar."

"Sensible woman," he muttered. When she frowned, he said, "It's the only way to drink decent coffee. I have mine flown in from the Kona Coast in Hawaii.''

"How nice for you," she said under her breath, mentally contrasting his freedom to order coffee from halfway across the Pacific with her own need to watch every penny to provide for baby Joel and herself. Most of her savings had been spent easing Ellen's last months, as well as paying the many medical bills that hadn't been covered by her sister's insurance, so being broke was a way of life for her these days.

As a computer consultant, usually she was well paid, but since Ellen's death, the hours she could work had been restricted by the need to care for Joel. It was one reason why she had jumped at helping Miranda for a couple of weeks. Not only could she take the baby to the office with her, but the salary was helping to cover some of the endless stream of bills.

Haley's mother and stepfather, Greg, had helped as much as they could, but they were both hopeless with money so most of the burden fell on Haley herself. She hadn't grudged her sister anything that had eased her final months, but she didn't appreciate the reminder that Sam Winton could have helped if he'd wanted to.

"I didn't catch that," he said, drawing her back to the present. "Don't you like Hawaiian coffee?"

"I...uh...said it's very nice," she improvised. All of a sudden she felt a pressing need to get out of there before she threw something at Sam. What had possessed her to think any good would come of meeting

Sam face-to-face? When Ellen had told him she was
expecting his baby, he hadn't exactly welcomed her
with open arms. The opposite, in fact. According to
Ellen, he had told her in no uncertain terms that he
couldn't possibly be the father of her child and had
all but thrown her out of his house.

It tore at Haley to recall that Ellen's tumor had
been in remission for a whole year when she'd started
working with Sam as an illustrator for one of his
books. They would never know whether the remission
would have gone on if not for Ellen falling pregnant—and after seeing him, Haley didn't doubt that
Joel was Sam's baby—but the strain of pregnancy
hadn't helped. Ellen's life had ended one short month
after giving birth to Joel. Only seeing the joy the baby
had given her sister, eased Haley's grief. She knew
that Ellen wouldn't have wanted anything to be different.

Except Sam's reaction. Her sister had been devas-
tated by his rejection. After all her medical treat-
ments, Ellen had been so sure she couldn't become
pregnant that she hadn't taken any precautions. Ellen
hadn't gone into details, but Haley assumed that Sam
hadn't taken any, either. Despite the obvious fact
they'd slept together, he couldn't know Ellen very
well if he thought she was the type to have any doubts
about who had fathered her child.

He probably thought she had picked on Sam because of his fame and obvious wealth. Only Haley
knew that Ellen had given herself to Sam out of a

moment of acute loneliness and fear. She had been awaiting the results of her latest checkup.

Haley had heard the whole story late one night, several months after they'd learned that Ellen's illness was back, when her pain made sleep impossible. Hearing her toss and turn, Haley had gone in to see if she could help, not that there was much she or anyone could do, but talking was one way she could take Ellen's mind off her suffering for a little while.

After Ellen had been working with Sam for some time, she told Haley, she had arrived to find Sam methodically tearing to shreds the divorce papers he'd received in the mail that morning.

In turmoil herself as she waited for her doctor to call with the results of the checkup, she had been as averse to working as Sam and they had taken comfort in each other's company. He hadn't known why Ellen was so distressed but he'd sensed that she'd needed his arms as much as he'd needed hers. Joel had been the result.

Knowing what hell her half sister had gone through before she went into remission, Haley couldn't blame Ellen for taking what pleasure she could in the moment. She also knew her sister's instinct would have been to try to help Sam. She had always been a giving person.

Haley didn't blame The Beast for seeking comfort after receiving the cold, hard proof that his marriage was over. Haley knew only too well how it felt when a relationship blew apart. She had been seeing Richard Cross, a business associate, for a few months, and had thought they were becoming close, when he told her bluntly to choose between him and her sister's baby. She had felt as if her world had come to an end. There had been no real choice. She didn't regret choosing the baby. But it still hurt.

She couldn't do anything to hold Richard, even supposing she wanted to after his cruel ultimatum. But she could and did blame Sam for his coldhearted refusal to accept his share of responsibility for Ellen's baby. The thought gave Haley the strength to do the job Miranda had trusted her to do. Haley opened her brief case and took out a file. "I've changed my mind. I'd rather skip coffee and get on with the purpose of this meeting."

Sam gave a suit-yourself shrug. "I hope you don't mind if I have some. I've been working since five this morning." Without waiting for a reply, he disappeared into his office. Her anger notched higher as she heard the hiss of an espresso machine followed by the chink of a spoon against porcelain. Sam definitely didn't stint himself.

Apart from the luxury of an espresso machine in his office, the room around her screamed affluence from the Cedric Emmanuel etchings on the walls to the designer furnishings. Thinking of Joel back at the office with Miranda, Haley began to seethe. How dare Sam spoil himself while his son had so little?

When Sam returned, cup in hand, the rich aroma of the coffee teased at her nostrils. She wished she hadn't been so hasty in refusing some. Depriving herself wasn't going to bring Sam into line, and her prickly behavior just might make him suspicious of her real motives.

"Are you sure you won't change your mind?" he asked, setting his cup down on a side table.

"No, thank you," she said, astonished that she could actually speak through clenched teeth. She had known that meeting Sam wouldn't be a picnic, but she had never expected it to be this much of an ordeal. Nor that it would bring back so much of the past tragic year, when she'd nursed Ellen through her pregnancy, knowing that her illness had recurred.

She had had to put her grief at losing her sister aside to take care of the baby. She had come to look upon Joel as her own child. Her anger at Sam was precisely because she now thought of Joel as her baby, she realized. There was no way she could be as objective as she wanted to be—as Miranda needed her to be—so they'd better get this over with before she said something she would regret. "I'd like to get down to business."

He prowled to the couch and sat beside her, so close, their thighs were within a whisper of touching. "Not until you tell me why you're so angry with me," he insisted. The invasion of her personal space was the last straw.

Yet anger was the last thing she felt when he was practically touching her, she found to her astonishment. What she felt was insanely, vibrantly aroused, and it was not how she wanted to feel around him.

"What makes you think I'm angry?" she asked,

managing to keep her voice steady with an effort that made her teeth ache.

"A writer's instinct for reading people," he said. "My guess is, you can barely restrain yourself from throwing something at me, and I'd like to know why. It can't be because I growled at you over the intercom. I was still in midscene and when I'm writing, I can be a real bear. Miranda must have warned you about me."

She shook her head, taking refuge in the truth. "I got the impression you're one of her favorite clients."

He smiled and the change was dramatic. She felt as if someone had turned on a sunlamp in the room, and actually found herself leaning toward him as if to the source of the energy. She pulled back with an effort. "Mine is a personal problem."

The word "personal" would have been enough to deter most men. But Sam looked interested. "Personal as in a man?"

Without meaning to, she had hooked the writer in him, she saw. She would have to be more careful. "I really don't think—"

"My point exactly," he cut in. "You can't think straight when you're preoccupied with another matter. Do I remind you of this man who's on your mind?"

If he only knew. She tried to keep her face impassive. Sam was too intuitive to accept an outright denial. "Perhaps."

"It would explain the displaced antagonism," he said as if to himself. "Sorry, analyzing people is a hobby of mine, as it is with most writers."

"But you're a children's writer."

He looked affronted. "My readers still expect believable characters with convincing motivation. The only difference is that my stories are written at an appropriate level of vocabulary."

"I didn't mean to suggest anything else."

His shoulders lifted. "I'm used to it. Demeaning children's literature is a spectator sport for some people. Do you have children of your own, Haley?"

"I hardly see—"

"That it's any of my business?" he finished for her. "You're probably right, but if we're to be on the same wavelength, I need to know more about you."

If it was a line, it was as smooth as silk, Haley thought. No wonder Ellen had found him so easy to fall for. Luckily she wasn't going to make the same mistake. "All you need to know about me is that Miranda sent me to take care of your staffing needs."

"Precisely," he concluded. "So, do you have children?"

He was impossible. "Yes," she snapped. Anything to get the discussion back on track.

"Boys? Girls?"

How old did he think she was? "Boy, singular. I'm only twenty-three myself. Joel is six months old, so you won't find him standing in line for your autograph."

Sam seemed unruffled. "He's a bit young for my books," he agreed, "Although hopefully they'll still be around when he starts reading."

This wasn't getting her anywhere. She made herself

remember Miranda's script. "I'm sure they will," she said in what was supposed to be a flattering tone.

He saw right through it. "This man you're so mad at, is he Joel's father?"

This, at least, she could answer truthfully. "Yes, he is."

She felt his gaze settle on the third finger of her left hand. "You're not married to him?"

Cursing herself for not thinking to wear a ring as camouflage, she snapped, "I should hope not."

Her vehemence intrigued him, she saw. "You have a child by him but you don't want him in your life. Interesting."

She tried to tell herself it was the writer in him, finding story possibilities in everything, but she didn't like the way his interest threatened to undermine her anger. "I don't want to talk about me," she said shortly. She was alarmed at the way the conversation kept coming back to her, when the whole point was to learn as much as she could about him so she could share it with Joel when he was old enough to ask about his father.

Her body had its own ideas, she found to her dismay. Sam sat so close that her senses were assailed by the woody fragrance of his aftershave lotion, coupled with the indefinable man-scent of Sam himself. The combination was relaxed and outdoorsy, not sophisticated like Richard, she thought, unwillingly comparing Richard with the man beside her. Sam's aura was so overpoweringly alluring it was in danger of throwing her completely off balance. Richard had never affected her so strongly.

She wasn't planning on dating Sam, she reminded herself hastily. After Richard, she enjoyed being accountable to no one but herself and Joel. So it hardly mattered whether Sam was the indoor or outdoor type, or given to group orgies behind his impressive wrought-iron gates.

Now where had that thought come from? What was it about him that made her thoughts turn in directions they had no business going? She and Richard had only split up a few weeks ago, so it wasn't as if she were starved for a man's attention.

The image of Sam's savagely rumpled bed returned to her mind. She kept a rein on her runaway thoughts by reminding herself that he had slept with her half sister, made her pregnant then denied that the baby could possibly be his.

Sobering as the reminder was, still she had trouble keeping her mind focused. Was this what he had done to Ellen?

It wasn't hard to see how it could happen, Haley thought. She pulled herself together with an effort. Sam might well be the kind of man who attracted women as effortlessly as a magnet attracted iron filings, but Haley had no intention of falling prey to his allure.

There was probably a good reason for his divorce, she told herself. Being the kind person she was, Ellen had accepted his explanation that he and his wife were simply incompatible, but Haley would have

wanted to dig deeper. Was he a workaholic or a wom-
anizer? Insanely jealous? That the fault could have
been on his ex-wife's side, she didn't want to think.
It brought her dangerously close to feeling compassion for him, and look where that had gotten Ellen!

For Joel's sake Haley knew she had to keep a clear
head and the best way to do that was to remind herself
that he was The Beast and he wasn't about to turn
into a handsome prince any time soon. Had it been
possible, he would surely have done so when Ellen
had told him about the baby. Instead, he had rejected
both her and their child. Haley made herself remember that part.

"I'd say your child is highly relevant to our discussion, if you're to be my house sitter while I'm on
tour," he said, breaking into her thoughts.

"You misunderstand," she said primly. "I'm only
interviewing you about your requirements, not taking
the job myself."

"Why not? You're not Miranda's regular assistant.
What happened to the pretty redhead with the infec-
tious laugh? Donna—isn't that her name?"

Telling herself she didn't care that he obviously
found Miranda's assistant attractive, Haley nevertheless found great satisfaction in saying, "I'm only filling in while Donna's on her honeymoon. She eloped
with a client."

She had surprised him, she saw, when his dark eyebrows arched upward. Serve him right if he had fancied Donna and she had run off with someone else.
It was time he got a taste of his own medicine. At

the same time, something uncomfortably like jealousy gripped her. What would it be like to be the object of his passion?

"Is she coming back?" he asked.

Didn't the man ever give up? "She'll be back in a few days with her new husband." She gave the relationship extra emphasis to make sure he got the point.

"What will happen to you when she does?"

Had she misread his concern? For a moment she'd thought he was sufficiently interested in Donna not to care whether or not she was married, as long as she was coming back. Now it sounded as if he was anxious about Haley herself. She didn't want his concern and she certainly didn't need it, she told herself, but found it more pleasant than she wanted to. "She'll return to her job and I'll go back to my own work."

"And that is?"

She didn't want to talk about herself but he gave her little option. "I'm a systems planning consultant for small companies who don't have full-time support staff. I organize their offices and their computer systems for maximum efficiency. Now can we—"

"Give me a minute to think." He massaged his chin, looking thoughtful. From the aura of aftershave around him, he had evidently shaved this morning but his hair was so black that a hint of shadow already darkened his jaw, giving him a slightly piratical air. "Organizational skills and Miranda's recommendation. You could be just the person I need. Last month my personal assistant left for Zimbabwe. I've been on a deadline so I haven't had chance to replace him yet.''

It explained the chaos in the office, she thought. ''Miranda understood you needed a house sitter.''

''I do, while I'm on tour with the new book. But it would be a great help if the same person could sort out the office for me while I'm gone.''

This wasn't going according to Miranda's script at all. In desperation, Haley pulled a clipboard out of her briefcase and consulted the points listed on it. ''All the same, the decision isn't up to me.''

''But it is up to me and if I decide you're right for this job, Miranda won't argue. She knows I pay well.'' He named a fee that Haley knew was in excess of Miranda's usual rates. Even taking out Miranda's commission, the amount left would solve a lot of Haley's problems.

It wouldn't solve the main one, that he was Joel's father, she told herself. All the same she couldn't help thinking that working for him would give her a heaven-sent chance to find out more about him so she could tell her child when the time came. Knowing his father and having regular contact with him would have been preferable, but that wasn't going to happen as long as Sam denied fathering Joel.

Haley knew only too well how it felt to grow up without really knowing your father. She still couldn't fathom how her mother, the most scatterbrained woman on earth, had managed to marry a strait-laced history professor and have his child. They had parted when Haley was six, and her mother had remarried an entomologist who was as eccentric as his wife. Currently the two of them were somewhere in the Amazon jungle collecting butterflies for his work. She had last seen Greg and her mother when they'd come back to Australia to attend their daughter's funeral.

Afterward her mother had stayed behind to help Haley, but within a couple of weeks she had created such chaos that Haley had decided she would cope better alone. Lovingly but firmly, she'd encouraged her mother to return to Greg in the jungle. She had suspected her mother was only too happy to comply. They loved each other but they had completely different ways of managing their lives.

Haley knew she took after her real father, who was the organized one in the family. Ellen had teased Haley about being able to put her hand on whatever she needed, while Ellen had inherited Greg's talent for creating disorder. Haley had tried to help her sister get organized, but it had never worked for long. "Let's face it, I take after my Dad and you take after yours," Ellen had conceded, throwing up her hands.

Haley had to agree. She'd seen little of her father while she was growing up but she had seen enough to know how finicky he was. In her teens, she had attempted to get to know him, but even she found his fussiness daunting. Arriving so much as five minutes late earned her his disapproval. She could only imagine his reaction if she had, say, spilled her food or used the wrong cutlery. She had been careful to do neither, but it hadn't exactly made for relaxing parent-child interactions.

To be fair, her father had tried to live up to her expectations, but their meetings always felt stilted and uncomfortable. It hurt to think her father knew more about Bess Tudor than Haley Glen and that he wasn't going to change. It seemed their orderliness was about all they had in common.

After one such outing, he had said, "I'm truly sorry I can't give you what you want, or know what to say to you. I don't know the first thing about being a good father. You're better off without me."

She had cried for two days afterward, then decided to accept the situation and get on with her life. She was proud of what she'd achieved, putting a down-payment on a her own apartment and setting herself up as her own boss. But it didn't stop the black moments, when she wondered what it was about her that her father had found so difficult to love, from coming. She wanted better for Joel, she thought fiercely. He wasn't going to have the same black moments in his life if she could do something about it. Even if it meant taking Sam's assignment herself.

She had seen enough of him already to be fairly sure that his mind wasn't easily changed once he had made it up. It sounded as if he wasn't about to budge about having her as his house sitter. Since she couldn't do much about it without letting Miranda down, she decided she might as well make the most of the chance to fulfill her mission. But first she needed to be sure that he wouldn't consider any other option.

"Can we at least go through the formalities?" she asked.

He looked pleased with himself. "Go ahead, as long as the name at the foot of that impressive checklist turns out to be yours."

She started to ask questions and tick boxes, uncomfortably aware that she was as interested in him as much for herself as for her baby.

When she closed the file, he grinned at her and she crumbled inside. It was easier to remember him as The Beast when he scowled at her. Then she didn't have this strange sensation of being swept out of her depth by a king tide.

"I was right, wasn't I?" he asked.

Her confusion was genuine. "About what?"

"After filling in all those little boxes, you're still perfect for the job."

"How can you possibly know? You know nothing about me." And he wouldn't, if she had anything to do with it. Her blood ran cold at the prospect of him linking her with Ellen and treating her—and her sister's baby—as cruelly.

"I don't need to know any more. By the time you move in, I'll be heading off on the tour. So we'll only be together long enough for me to brief you on what needs doing, then you'll have the place to yourself."

She could swear he sounded disappointed, but told herself the strain of the meeting was making her imagine things. "You don't have a problem with a baby staying in your house."

His expression darkened. "My sister, Jessie, has

two small children so the house is equipped for a baby. And in my line of work, I'm unlikely to have a problem with children.''

Only with Joel, she thought, quelling her reaction. ''I could refuse to take the assignment.''

''But you won't.''

She met his penetrating blue gaze with an equally direct one of her own. ''What makes you so sure?''

''Because you don't want to lose Miranda one of her best clients.''

With sinking heart, Haley knew that he had won.

Chapter Two

As she drove between the gates to Sam's house, a curious feeling of homecoming overcame Haley. She told herself it was because this was her second visit, but knew it had more to do with the suitcases packed around the baby seat. They made her feel as if she was staying longer than the couple of weeks Sam required.

This time she didn't get out of the car right away, but waited until Sam emerged and spoke to Dougal, although the dog was wagging its tail furiously, rather than barking a warning.

"Good morning," she said, annoyed at the heat she felt surge into her face at the sight of Sam. Dressed in dark blue pants and a white summer-weight sweater, he looked less like The Beast of her sister's experience and more like the kind of man Haley herself could be attracted to if she was crazy enough to let it happen.

He looked as uncomfortable as she felt. Maybe he just didn't like babies, she thought as she unstrapped Joel from his baby seat. If so, he should have thought about that before getting Ellen pregnant.

"You're late," he said.

Haley frowned at him, stung by his tone. "I understood from Miranda that you don't have to leave until this afternoon, so there's plenty of time for you to brief me." She was late because Joel had burbled strained turkey all over her best blouse, forcing her to change into a T-shirt before she could set off, but she didn't say so. She felt unprofessional enough, arriving for a job with a baby and a mountain of possessions in tow, most of them to do with Joel's care. "If you'll show me my room, I'll settle the baby down for a nap, then you can give me my instructions."

He bounded down the front steps and picked up her largest suitcase as if it weighed nothing at all, then loaded his other arm with an assortment of possessions. His eyebrows rose. "What do you pack when you're going away for a month?"

"Babies need a lot of things."

His smile vanished as if a lightbulb had been switched off. "I wouldn't know," he said shortly, and started back up the steps.

She stared after his rigid back in consternation. What had she said? He couldn't be upset because she'd arrived with the baby. He'd known from the beginning that they were a package, but he obviously didn't want to have anything to do with Joel. He hadn't even acknowledged the baby's presence, she thought furiously. "He is a person, you know," she snapped.

Sam froze on the top step, regarding her with an expression like thunder. "Excuse me?"

It was too late to close her fool mouth now, so she said, "Sam, this is Joel. Joel, this is Sam. Say hello to Joel, Sam."

He looked as if he would rather strip naked on the step, an image that startled her because of the vivid way it sprang into her mind. Not somewhere she had any business going, she told herself as he said through clenched teeth, "Hello, Joel."

"See? That wasn't so hard, was it?"

Harder than she knew, Sam thought. Everything in him protested at the sight of the baby waving chubby arms at him, a living reminder of Sam's own inadequacy. When he'd hired Haley, he'd been sure he could cope with her child living under his roof. He hadn't expected the baby's arrival to trigger a rush of paternal longing so strong it was like a physical pain.

Suddenly Haley thrust the child at him. "Now you've been introduced, would you mind holding Joel while I fetch his favorite toy? I just remembered I left it in the car."

Before Sam could say a word she bounded back down the steps, leaving him with the baby. As the child's scents engulfed him and the small hands clutched at him, Sam felt his stomach muscles twist.

Joel looked exactly how Sam had imagined his own son would look before he discovered that it would never happen, and his heart felt as if it was being crushed in a giant hand.

Joel opened his mouth to protest. Instinctively Sam jiggled the baby up and down in his arms, and the child's cry dropped to a whimper. "Hey now, she'll be back in a minute," Sam assured Joel. "We men can cope on our own for a short time, can't we?"

Sam's serious tone caught Joel's attention. The whimpers faded altogether and the baby fixed Sam with huge, luminous eyes. Then he reached for the top button of Sam's shirt and tugged on it.

Immediately Sam felt an answering tug deep inside, and his hold on the baby tightened as regret speared through him. He'd held babies before. His sister, Jessie, had two. But when they were born, Sam had still believed he would father children of his own someday. Now he knew it was impossible, and holding Joel heightened the aching sense of loss that was never far from Sam's mind.

"Not your fault, cute stuff," Sam said, hearing his voice sound husky with emotion. "You're just the sort of kid I always hoped I'd have."

Sam had Joel's full attention. The baby hung onto Sam's shirt and gave every sign of listening intently. "Yep, I wanted one just like you and one just like…" Sam caught himself about to say "your mother" and substituted, "…well, a little girl."

At the word "girl," Joel made muttering noises. Sam felt a smile start. "Don't like girls, huh? You'll change your tune one day, when you meet that special lady you can't live without. I thought I'd found her in my ex-wife, Christine,'' he explained to the baby. Joel's head bobbed as if he understood every word, although Sam knew he couldn't possibly. "Not that we're the best example. She was a cover model I met at my publishers' Christmas party. 'Course it doesn't have to turn out the way it did for us,'' Sam went on, wondering if he'd gone completely crazy. Why was he telling this to a *baby,* for goodness sake? But Joel made a good listener, and Sam's monologue was keeping the baby calm, so he decided it didn't matter what he said, as long as he used a soothing tone.

"She said she didn't mind that I couldn't father children,'' he went on in a monotone. "Even had her big shot doctor brother do the tests so we could keep the news in the family. Never did like me, her brother. Thought a writer wasn't good enough for his sister. Medically speaking, he was right.''

Joel smacked him in the chest. "Bab-bab.''

"Yeah, pretty bad,'' Sam agreed. "But then I can't stand my ex's brother either, so we're even. But you don't want to hear this. Heck, I don't want to hear this.''

"Hear what?'' Haley asked, bounding up the steps. Under her arm she carried a woolly lamb toy. Joel's eyes lit up at the sight of his plaything and he reached out.

As she took the baby from him, Sam felt a twinge of remorse. "Men's business,'' he said gruffly, annoyed with himself for letting the baby get to him.

He hadn't been prepared for the way Haley made him feel, either. Watching her settle the child on one hip, Sam felt flames leap inside him.

His sister, Jessie, claimed that the only good thing about being pregnant was the way her breasts filled out. Despite her recent motherhood, Haley's breasts were still small, but they were in scale with the rest of her trim figure, Sam decided. She wore a wrap-around skirt of Oriental-looking material in black and gold, with a black T-shirt that clung to her curves as if poured on. In her arms, the baby fisted a handful of the T-shirt and held on. Sam almost groaned aloud.

Joining them on the steps, Dougal barked and the baby's eyes widened. Haley bent down, allowing the dog to sniff the infant. "Friend, Dougal," she said firmly. The dog's tail bannered and he gave the baby's hand a gentle lick. Joel gurgled with delight, a smile breaking out on his chubby face. He caught a handful of the dog's fur and pulled, but Dougal seemed to sense that he wasn't to respond and stood like a statue. Carefully, Haley untangled the baby's hand and straightened. Dougal glued himself to her side as if he had every intention of staying there for the next two weeks.

"Much more of that and he won't want to know me," Sam said, telling himself he wasn't bothered by the dog's apparent defection. Sure, he wasn't. Any more than he was bothered by the Madonna-and-child image in front of him. Or the empty way his arms felt when Haley took the baby from him.

She looked up and smiled, and the sun came out.

"Dogs have plenty of affection to go around. I'm just glad that Joel isn't scared of him."

Sam had promised himself he wouldn't get involved with either Haley or her child, but would settle them in their quarters, brief her on what she was to do while he was away, then get the dickens out of here. Suddenly he felt a powerful urge to stick around. "Joel doesn't look as if he's scared of anything," he said.

"Thunderstorms," she admitted, jiggling the baby on her hip. "You don't like bad old storms, do you, pumpkin?"

"He's scared of storms?"

She nodded. A thunderstorm had been raging the night Ellen passed away and Haley couldn't help wondering if the baby associated storms with the loss of his mother. She told herself he was far too young and, anyway, most babies disliked loud noises, but she found the connection curious.

Sam used the heavy case to wedge the front door open so she could carry the baby inside. As she passed him in the narrow opening, her hip brushed his. It was the slightest contact, nothing really, but awareness of him vibrated through her, leaving her breathless. This would have to stop. He was The Beast, remember? The baby in her arms ought to remind her, if she needed it.

Sam followed her inside and put her possessions down on the polished parquet floor while he closed the door. "Joel isn't the only one. I was scared of thunderstorms when I was a boy."

She knew her expression betrayed her surprise. He looked too overwhelmingly masculine and sure of himself to be scared of anything. "You were?"

He nodded. "When I was four, lightning struck a tree outside my bedroom window, severing a branch that crashed into my room, missing my bed by inches. I hated storms for years afterwards."

The image of a terrified little boy lying in his bed while a storm raged around him filled her mind. Much as she hated to feel compassion for him, it was impossible not to. "Anyone would feel the same after that."

"I outgrew it. Joel probably will, too."

Suddenly she became aware of how close they were standing, almost within kissing distance, she thought, astonishing herself. How would it feel to have his generously proportioned mouth covering hers? Feathers of sensation whispered along her spine and she closed her eyes, the feel of his lips so palpable that her own parted in response.

She opened her eyes in amazement. What was going on here? She was suddenly glad that the baby in her arms provided a tangible barrier between them. Sam was the last man in the world she should fantasize about kissing.

She became aware that he was speaking to her. "I've put you in my room."

"You've what?"

"*Your* room while I'm away," he said, heading off her objection. "It has a separate dressing room large enough to make a nursery for Joel."

"Oh, thanks." How much more foolish could one woman feel? For a minute she'd thought... She drove the idea away by reminding herself that she was here to do a job. Perhaps not the one that Sam had hired her to do, but a job nonetheless.

If Sam suspected her real agenda, he wouldn't offer her any hospitality, far less the use of his own room for herself and Joel, she knew. Reminding herself that Sam had left her no alternative if she was to obtain justice for Joel didn't entirely appease her conscience. The sight of the baby's angelic features helped Haley to harden her heart. Sam had not only rejected his son, but in profiting from Ellen's idea for the Cosmic Panda character, Sam had robbed Joel of his birthright as well. All Haley needed was proof, and she meant to find it while Sam was away.

Her sister had told Haley the bare bones of the story. As a book illustrator, Ellen had met Sam at a publishing dinner three years before, and she had ended up sketching ideas on the back of a menu. According to Ellen, that was when Cosmic Panda was born.

Haley didn't know what would have happened if Ellen hadn't become ill six months after giving Sam the idea for the character. Ellen hadn't wanted anyone to know how ill she was, and Sam had promised to let her work with him on future Panda books as soon as she recovered. Being Ellen, she had put the work before her own welfare, and had urged Sam to hire another artist in the meantime. The first book had been published to great acclaim. The only name on it was Sam's.

He had kept his word about hiring Ellen to illustrate the second Panda book when she let him know she was working again. But Haley had read all the publicity, looking in vain for him to give her sister any of the credit. Although plainly disappointed, Ellen had insisted she didn't want a fuss made. While Ellen lived, Haley had felt bound to abide by her sister's wishes. Now she was free of that obligation.

As soon as she had evidence that the character had been Ellen's creation, Haley intended to confront Sam with what she knew. The price Haley wanted for keeping the news to herself was Sam's acknowledgment of Joel as his son. A fair exchange, really. If Haley had to wrestle her conscience over how she brought it about, so be it.

Her thoughts were interrupted when Sam opened a door off the wide corridor and gestured for her to enter. It was the bedroom she had glimpsed the day she came for the interview, but it looked far neater today. The massive four-poster was made and every surface gleamed.

There was a walk-in closet with several railings cleared so she could hang her own clothes. Another door led to a smaller, light-filled room set up as the nursery, she saw when she went inside. She ran a hand over the glowing timber of the rocking chair. At her touch it moved slightly. Then she caught sight of the hand-carved crib and gave an involuntary gasp of pleasure. "It's beautiful. I brought Joel's portable crib but this is much nicer. I've never seen one like it. Is it very old?"

"Family heirloom," he said. "I dug it out of the attic for you." He didn't add that his sister had supplied the sheets and blankets and a few other baby things she had to spare, although not without a considerable amount of teasing. She had been convinced that he fancied the baby's mother.

The trouble was, he did. He had never been so diverted by a woman before. Yet for some reason, she didn't like him. He knew it as well as he knew his own name. Occasionally she smiled at him in a way that turned his insides to jelly, then she seemed to remind herself that she wasn't supposed to like him, and the sun would go in. It was a mystery, and he didn't like mysteries.

The baby was another mystery, reminding him of someone he couldn't quite place. Telling himself that all babies looked alike didn't help.

Haley shot him a concerned glance. "You've gone to a lot of trouble."

"I could hardly let Joel sleep in the bottom drawer of a chest."

But he could deny fathering the baby, the thought tempering her pleasure at the preparations he had made. She placed the baby into the crib while she got herself organized. "It's time for Joel's nap," she said. "I'll have to change him first and I warn you, it's not a pretty sight."

She was doing it again, he saw, freezing him out for no good reason he could fathom. He also resented her assumption that he couldn't handle a baby's basic needs. Hadn't he rustled up the crib and other necessities? "For your information, I've had some practice taking care of my sister's two babies so I'm not likely to be offended by anything that comes out of either end. But since I'm obviously in your way, I'll leave you to it. When you're finished, join me in the library and we'll go over what I want you to do. It's the last room at the end of the hall."

"I remember where it is. I won't be long."

"Take your time. As you reminded me, I have a couple of hours up my sleeve. You might like to settle in first."

"Thank you, I would."

Her tone would have frosted a martini glass, he thought. At the door, he turned back. "What did I do to make you so mad at me?"

Her eyes betrayed her shock as she looked up from digging through a bag of baby things. "I don't know what you mean."

"At the interview, you admitted being mad at Joel's father, and his absence suggests you have a right to be, but is that any reason to take it out on me? Or do you just dislike men in general?"

She unrolled a thick pad on top of a chest and lifted the baby onto it before saying, "I don't dislike men."

"Then it must be me."

In the act of undressing Joel, she paused. "What makes you think I don't like you?"

"Your attitude hardly makes you a charter member of the Sam Winton Fan Club."

"I didn't realize it was a qualification for your house sitter."

"You're dodging the question."

Her hands stilled again as she gave him a look of exasperation. "I don't know the answer. I hardly know *you*."

"It wouldn't be hard to remedy."

He assumed she wanted a remedy, Haley told herself. She didn't, did she? She only wanted justice for Joel. Thinking of her reaction to the idea of kissing Sam, she knew she would have to be careful not to lose sight of her goal. "I'll bear it in mind," she said.

He looked as if he wanted to say more, then seemed to think better of it, closing the door behind him with such exaggerated care that she was sure it was only to stop himself from slamming it.

What was the matter with him, she asked herself as she removed the baby's clothes, then dabbed and wiped and powdered, so accustomed to the task that she hardly thought about the steps any more. Usually she used the time to play with Joel, but she was too distracted to do more than make reassuring noises. He didn't seem to mind. He was too fascinated by a mobile of brightly colored circus clowns and animals hanging from the ceiling. Where had Sam found that? It didn't look like an heirloom from his attic.

He had mentioned that his sister had children. She could have contributed the mobile and some of the other baby items, Haley concluded. It was a lot to do for someone who was only staying for a couple of weeks.

She thought about his question. Did she hate Sam? She had told herself she did, for the way he had treated Ellen. But he was making it surprisingly hard to do. "Why did he have to fix everything up so nicely for us?" she asked Joel.

The baby kicked and cooed, and she sighed. "You don't know the answer any more than I do, pumpkin." She glanced at the closed door. "Why can't your daddy act like the beast he is, then it would be easy to dislike him?"

"Da-da-da," the baby gurgled.

She looked at him suspiciously. "Are you trying to say daddy? It's too soon, isn't it?"

"Da-da-da," he repeated.

She felt a sudden flash of jealousy and gathered the now sweet-smelling infant into her arms. "Can you say mama?"

The baby blew a bubble at her and thrust his fingers into her mouth. "Ba."

"Mama," she repeated patiently around his fingers.

"Ba. Ba."

"Ma-ma," she tried again, then realized that her friend had dozed off in midword. It was probably just as well. It had been a busy morning for Joel, and she was sure the tension between herself and Sam wasn't helping. Joel didn't stir when she placed him in the crib and tucked a soft blanket around him. She retrieved his woolly lamb toy from the table, and placed it at the foot of the crib where he would see it if he awoke.

"Sweet dreams," she whispered, kissing the tip of her finger and touching his forehead. She never tired of watching the baby sleep, but she didn't want to keep Sam waiting. Despite his invitation to take her time, she decided to leave the unpacking until she had the house to herself.

Sam wasn't in the library when she got there, but the door to his office stood open and she heard furious muttering coming from it. Curious, she walked in. Sam was frowning over his computer. His hair was disheveled where he'd evidently thrust his fingers through it. He looked every inch a writer and he looked gorgeous.

"Problem?" she asked.

He looked up, as if her arrival had startled him. "New scriptwriting program. Darned thing won't load properly. Cosmic Panda has been optioned as a TV series and I need the program to write the script," he explained. "That's privileged information, by the way. My agent plans to announce it publicly after the tour."

Hearing that the character he had purloined from Ellen was about to become even more profitable helped her to harden her heart against the urge to go to him and smooth away the lines of worry creasing his brow.

Remembering why he had hired her, she asked, "Do you need the program before you go?" When he shook his head, she said, "Then leave it and I'll load it for you."

"I knew you were the person I needed."

His words and electric smile of gratitude undermined her resolve, and her pulse double-timed as his dark gaze rested on her. "What?"

"You have baby powder on your nose."

She scrubbed at it with the back of her hand then winced. "Some of it went into my eye."

He uncoiled from the desk and stood up. "Here, let me help."

With the grace and purpose of a mountain lion, he stalked to her side and put an arm around her shoulder to pull her closer to the window, into the light. Tilting her head back, he studied her eye for a moment, then released the lid. "Your eye looks clear now. You've probably scratched it and that's why it feels as if something's still there. If you bathe it, the pain will go away."

"It's gone now." The words came out as a strangled whisper, so aware was she of his touch. She tried to shake herself free of his spell and move away, but her legs felt frozen. Only her mind was vibrantly active, processing how much she liked the feel of his arm around her and the brush of his fingers against her face.

So when he bent his head and kissed her, it felt completely natural and right. Her mouth trembled under his, but she couldn't summon the will to stop him. Sighing softly, she closed her eyes, seeing stars behind her closed lids as he sipped and nuzzled, touched and tasted.

For such a powerful man, he was gentle, never once taking undue advantage of her startled acquiescence. At the slightest objection from her, he would have released her, she sensed. *So say something, stop this,* her logical brain urged. She kept silent.

Yet inside her ran a riot of responses that made her blood leap and her heart gather speed. His fingers slid along her jaw, gently caressing, until he reached the pulse at her throat. She felt him register it and wished she could stop the betraying hammering. But she could no more control it than she could tear her mouth away from his. If anything, she wanted more, hungered for it, and the shameful whimper of pleasure she couldn't restrain told him so.

Almost of its own accord, her hand wound around his neck, pulling his face against hers so she could taste him more deeply. The tiny hairs on the back of his neck teased her palm and her splayed fingers slid up into his hair, tangling in the silken strands, the way her mind tangled in the sensations he was arousing with his clever mouth. Shivers took her. She had been kissed often enough to know that it could be much more than this gentle exploration, and to her shame, she wanted everything he was capable of giving her.

Uneasiness gripped her. She couldn't possibly want this from The Beast. She had no business letting him kiss her, far less allowing herself to imagine what might come after it in time. Nothing would come of it because she didn't want it to.

Liar, whispered through her mind. From her very first sight of Sam, she had known that she wanted him. No matter how she cloaked her feelings in motives of revenge for Ellen and justice for Joel, she couldn't hide the truth from herself. In spite of all the reasons why it was wrong, Sam attracted her more strongly than any man had ever done.

She wasn't the only one feeling the power of attraction, she thought, knowing she didn't imagine his reluctance as he moved away from her. His breathing was as labored as hers, and his eyes were full of questions. She had no more answers for him than she had for herself. Her confused expression must have told him so because he gave a quick shake of his head. "I didn't mean to do that."

"Makes two of us," she murmured, still gripped by a feeling of arousal so intense it was almost painful. More painful still was the awareness that she was probably reading far more into the kiss than he was. She already knew he was capable of casual affairs. Her sister's experience was proof enough. But Haley knew she was not capable of anything casual where love was concerned. It simply wasn't in her nature. Even Richard's desertion had hurt her deeply, although she knew she was better off without him.

She was certainly better off without Sam.

Needing something to do while she recovered her composure, she moved to his desk and began straightening piles of papers, aware that they trembled in her hands like autumn leaves in a breeze. "I don't make a habit of letting strangers kiss me," she said shakily.

"Any more than I make a habit of kissing them."

She almost laughed out loud. He had found the one sure way to break the spell. "Of course not," she agreed, her tone brittle.

She watched his eyes narrow. "You sound as if you don't believe me."

Thinking of her sister, she suppressed a shiver. Joel

was ample proof of how readily Sam had taken a virtual stranger into his bed. Why should he let a little thing like a kiss bother him? "Why shouldn't I believe you?" she countered.

His speculative look slid over her. "I don't know. I get the darnedest feeling that you know a lot more about me than I know about you."

She turned away to hide her expression. He was more right than he knew, but her cover would be blown if she admitted it. She kept her tone light. "If I did know any more, it would hardly concern your love life, would it?"

To her relief he accepted the comment at face value. "True enough." He pushed a hand through his hair, obviously a habit he had developed that he seemed to be unaware of. "Sometimes I forget how much publicity I've had since my first book came out."

Haley welcomed the change of subject. "Have you always written children's books?"

He gave her a wry look. "Do you mean, have I ever written a real book?"

She let her affront show. "If I had, I'd have said so."

The storm that had threatened to break over his features cleared quickly. "Something tells me you would. And the answer is yes, I published three books on the work of the early Greek writers before starting to write for children. Studying Homer got me interested in the use of myths to explore and explain human nature, so my next young adult books were myth-based. Panda was a natural progression from that.''

He spoke with such conviction that she knew her first doubt. She had known that he used Cosmic Panda as a model to help children explore themselves and their lives. If he had really hatched the idea after studying Homer, then how could he have stolen it from her sister? She knew she wouldn't get much peace until she had the answer, and she wouldn't get it until she had the house to herself.

''If you're to leave on time, shouldn't we get started on what you want me to do?'' she suggested.

He nodded, seating himself at his desk. ''It shouldn't take long. I mainly want you to restore some order to my computer files.''

Glad to have the conversation safely on neutral ground, she said, ''You've backed up everything sensitive, I hope.''

His eyebrow canted upward. ''Don't you trust your own skills?''

She shook her head. ''I don't trust anything that depends on a power supply.''

''Then relax, everything's backed up. So you can do as you will with the computer, and the manual filing system. By the time I return, I expect my office to be a model of order and efficiency.''

She surveyed the chaos of files and papers around her. ''I'm an organizer, not a miracle worker.''

He rolled his eyes heavenward. ''And I specifically asked Miranda to send me an angel.''

She tossed her head. "What you see is what you get."

From where he sat, she looked angelic enough, he thought. The taste of her mouth lingered on his lips as he ran his tongue experimentally over them. He would give a lot to taste her again. It had taken all his willpower not to overdo things the first time, for fear of frightening her off.

He had meant it when he said the kiss wasn't planned. Oh, he had known he was going to kiss her from the moment he'd set eyes on her, but he hadn't expected it to happen so swiftly. Not that he was complaining. The brief taste was enough to convince him he wasn't imagining the strength of the chemistry sizzling between them.

She felt it too, he could swear. But she was wary of him, although he couldn't think why, since their paths had never crossed before as far as he knew. So he didn't want to do anything she wasn't ready for.

Unfortunately, he wasn't usually a patient man. At a young age, he had learned the hard way that life was too short to defer anything that really mattered. And although she didn't know it yet, Haley mattered to him. They would be good together, he was positive. She already had a baby, so his problem wasn't likely to bother her. Although she hadn't talked about it, he guessed that her experience with the baby's father hadn't been good, so she wasn't looking for marriage, any more than he was. It was a match made in Heaven.

If she hadn't agreed to work for him, he would

have had to find some other way to see her again. Having her safely under his roof simplified things, but it would be frustrating not to be under it at the same time

As he stood to take her on a tour of the rest of the house, his hand brushed the small of her back and the instant tightening in his loins made him think it wasn't such a bad thing if circumstances ensured they kept some distance for the moment.

At least until she was ready to accept that she would be his sooner or later. Sooner, he hoped. Later, if she required considerable courting. He would even enjoy it, and he would make sure she enjoyed it, too. As long as the end result was the same. Haley Glen in his bed, her glorious hair mussed and her skin glowing with the aftermath of their lovemaking.

Chapter Three

It had been an extraordinary day, Haley mused as she lay in Sam's vast bed, too stimulated to sleep and too worn out not to. After they had finished going over what needed to be done in his office, he had taken her on a tour of the house, explaining where everything was kept and how the security system worked. Then he had driven off with what she could swear was reluctance. To her dismay, she felt it too. Watching him leave, she had felt as if she was losing something important.

That was crazy, surely? She barely knew the man, and what she did know of him wasn't promising. *Letting him kiss you wasn't your brightest move,* she told herself. It had complicated things, making her see him in a different light. Not as The Beast who deserved her anger and scorn, but as a man who could make her senses run riot with his slightest touch.

She ran her tongue over her lips, slightly surprised to find they weren't swollen or bruised, when they felt as if they should be both. A kiss had never affected her so powerfully before. Could she have stopped him from kissing her? Without a doubt. He hadn't forced her into anything. Had she wanted to? Not in a million years.

Haley tried to feel glad he was gone. No more temptation. No more kisses, either. But that was a good thing, right? So why couldn't she fall asleep? She was tired enough. She smiled into the darkness as she imagined Ellen's comments if she knew that Haley had already finished unpacking.

"Can't help yourself, can you? Are you sure you don't want to scrub the bathroom while you're at it?" her sister would have teased. Arguing that it wouldn't be necessary because Sam's house was untidy but spotlessly clean wouldn't have silenced Ellen. The trouble was, it was true, Haley couldn't help herself. She couldn't relax until she'd put everything away and arranged Joel's room to her liking. As a result, she had worn herself out.

Sometimes she wished she had inherited some other trait from her father than his passion for order, but didn't find it surprising. When her father and mother lived together, everything had been predictable, even the disagreements between them. Her earliest memories were of her father arguing from logic and reason, in a clipped voice she could still hear in her head if she concentrated, while her mother had resorted to screaming, weeping and in extremes, throwing things.

She still did, Haley thought, smiling to herself, except that her stepfather was inclined to throw things back. It cleared the air, but didn't make for peace and harmony. At such times, Haley had taken refuge in her own room, rearranging her things until they were in apple-pie order, feeling herself grow calmer in proportion to the neatness around her.

She had done the same the night Ellen died, she remembered. After doing everything that had to be done for her sister, she had cleaned the house from top to bottom, scrubbing every surface until her hands were raw and her fingernails ragged. Only then had she been able to go to bed, too exhausted even to cry.

What a difference Joel had made in her life, she mused. Sometimes she wondered if she was destined to become his mother, so she could learn that there were more important things in life than tidiness. It hadn't taken long. Although she still liked everything just so, she also accepted that no one could be obsessively orderly living with a baby.

Working in Sam's office was going to be a trial until she could restore some harmony to it, she thought. She would have to be careful not to get so caught up in the job he had hired her to do that she forgot her mission. It was the least she could do for Ellen's memory, and for Joel.

She was relieved that the baby had settled down without a fuss, tired out after their romp in the garden with Dougal after dinner. He and the dog seemed made for each other, the big, hairy hound as gentle as a lamb around the baby.

Picturing them together, she felt a warm glow of satisfaction. She had spread a blanket on the grass beneath a Moreton Bay fig tree. Dougal had sprawled across half of it and she had propped Joel against a cushion with his toys on the other half. Before long, the dog had wriggled closer to the baby who ended up using Dougal as a pillow.

It was as close as she was going to come to a happy family scene, she thought. The only thing missing was a father.

Impatient with herself, she sat up and thumped the feather pillow, hoping that reshaping it would help her get to sleep. Then she heard a noise and froze, listening intently. It had come from the front hallway.

It was probably just the house settling, or the refrigerator defrosting itself, although she shouldn't have been able to hear it from this part of the house. Dougal was outside, patroling the grounds, so it couldn't be the dog. Then the small hairs on the back of her neck rose as she heard the unmistakable sound of the front door opening and closing.

Her heart triple-timed. Someone was in the house. What was the matter with the alarm system? Why wasn't Dougal barking his head off? Had the intruder done something to silence the dog, and then disabled the alarm?

She groped for the telephone by her bedside then remembered that she wasn't in her own apartment. She was in Sam's room and the phone was a cordless model. Too late, she remembered leaving the handset on a dresser across the room after using it to call Miranda to assure her they had settled in nicely. So much for order and harmony, she thought, furious with herself. The one time she should have put something back in its place, she had neglected to do it and look at the consequences.

No intruder was going to harm a hair of her baby's head, she resolved. She threw back the covers. She remembered seeing an ornamental poker propped beside the fireplace. If she could get to it before the intruder reached her, it would make a perfect weapon.

She was feeling her way across the room when the door opened and a huge male figure filled the opening. Heart pounding, she lunged for the fireplace. Hefting the poker, she turned back, ready to do battle for her baby's sake, only to be blinded when the intruder snapped on the room light.

"What in the devil?"

"Sam, what are you doing here?"

He blinked in the strong light. "Oh blazes, I forgot I'd given you my room."

She became aware of how bizarre she must look, standing in the middle of the room in her nightgown, with a poker raised over her head. She lowered the heavy rod slowly. "You still haven't explained what you're doing here." The aftermath of fear made her voice thick with emotion, and her whole body vibrated like a tuning fork.

He became aware of her tone and posture. "I didn't mean to frighten you."

"You didn't frighten me, you scared me out of my wits." She was furious both with herself for sounding so pathetic and with him for causing it. But especially with herself, for the way her spirits leaped at the mere sight of him.

He rubbed his stubble-shadowed jaw. "I wasn't thinking straight. I was at the airport with my agent when we got word that the distributors have called a lightning strike and the books won't make it to the stores in time. The unionists won't let anyone cross the picket line, and they've dug in for a long fight, so we're at an impasse. I spent the last few hours trying to sort out the mess. In the end there was nothing to do but postpone the tour. I should have thought to call ahead and warn you."

"There are also hotels you could have gone to for the night," she said, hating the way her voice shook. She hated even more that it might be a reaction to his reappearance, rather than the aftermath of the fright he'd caused her.

"After the day I've had, a hotel doesn't hold much appeal." While she held far more, Sam acknowledged. He should have been furious about the strike, and the professional part of him had been. But the part wanting to hold her in his arms and kiss her again, was a good deal stronger.

He had stumbled to his room on autopilot. And he was sorry for scaring her. But he wasn't sorry for catching her in such beautiful disarray. Her hair tumbled around her shoulders, and her filmy gown clung to her lithe body. A thousand needs clawed at him.

She looked the way he'd imagined her, except that in his fantasy he had caused her disarray by making wild, passionate love to her. He hadn't planned on creating the effect by scaring her half to death.

He swallowed hard, fighting a surge of arousal. Couldn't he be around her for five minutes without her affecting him physically? Maybe it was the sight of the rumpled bed giving him ideas. *No,* he corrected the thought. *She* gave him ideas. The rumpled bed only made them harder to resist.

He had better get out of here before resistance became impossible. "I'll make up another room."

"Wait." He saw her fight an internal battle with herself. Again he had the strange sense that she was in two minds about him, as if she wanted to dislike him, but was finding it harder and harder to keep up. Good. It was progress of a sort, especially when she added, "You look like you could use a nightcap. I'll make it."

Common sense told him to refuse her offer while he still had some self-control. Pity he wasn't big on common sense. "Sounds good to me," he agreed.

She returned the poker to its place and picked up a robe.

While she bustled around his kitchen, he dropped his jacket over the back of a chair and loosened the collar of his shirt. Having Haley in the house made it seem homier, somehow. It bothered him how much he liked it. Wanting her in his bed and in his life were two different animals.

"Cocoa?" he asked, slightly bemused when she

put a steaming mug in front of him. Perched on a stool in the kitchen, he had been thinking fondly of a double Scotch with a Haley chaser. Cocoa was a long way from what he'd had in mind.

She rested both hands on the countertop. "Cocoa will help you to sleep. You look exhausted."

"It was a long day." He wrapped his hands around the mug, letting the warmth seep into him. It wasn't as comforting as wrapping his arms around her, but it was probably wiser.

He took a long swallow of the cocoa and found to his surprise that it tasted good. A little sweet, perhaps, but rich and satisfying. He hadn't drunk cocoa since his mother made it for him as a bedtime drink when he was a boy. These days he didn't keep any in the house, so Haley must have brought it with her.

She had pulled the robe on over the nightgown, but even swathed in satin, she looked good enough to eat. He forced himself to focus on the swirling pattern the cream made in the mug. They reminded him of the white flecks in her chocolate-colored eyes. "You don't have to keep me company," he said gruffly to hide how much he liked having her near.

She brought another mug to the breakfast bar, and perched on a stool opposite him. "It's all right, I had trouble getting to sleep, anyway."

"Being in a strange house?"

"Probably."

"I travel so much for the books that I can sleep anywhere," he told her, wondering why he wanted to share such trivia with her. As his sisters would testify, he normally gave away as little about himself as he could. Smarter than leaving yourself vulnerable.

It didn't stop him from wanting to get as close as he possibly could to this woman. "I suppose you've lived in the same house all your life."

She shook her head. "My parents split up when I was little. Then my mother remarried and we moved around a lot with my stepfather's work. My mother and stepfather think a home is adequate as long as it's watertight."

"Hippies?"

"Intellectuals, actually, more comfortable with things of the mind than the material world. My mother's a linguist and my stepfather is a respected entomologist. At this moment, they're in South America hunting for some rare beetle that is supposed to help cure cancer."

Sam looked thoughtful. "Maybe I've heard of him. My half sister is married to a bug man, too. It's such a close-knit profession, their paths have probably crossed."

"I doubt it," she said quickly, as if reluctant to establish any sort of connection with him. For a moment, she looked panicky, as if mentioning her family was a mistake. Why, he wondered? She added, "My stepfather hasn't worked in Australia for years. He and my mother only come home for R & R."

He told himself he was imagining her reaction. "No brothers or sisters?"

Her hands tightened their grip on the mug. "One sister. She died five months ago."

"I'm sorry." It sounded inadequate but he didn't know what else to say. She still felt her loss keenly, he saw, as her eyes misted over. It was all he could do not to take her in his arms and comfort her. At least, that would be his excuse.

"I'm sorry, too," she said, her expression accusing, as if he'd had something to do with her sister's death. It was nonsense, but he couldn't shake the feeling. Or maybe her problem was with all men. He returned to his earlier theory that Haley had a problem with men in general. Had one of his gender harmed her sister?

Learning more might give him a clue. "What was her name?"

"Ellen," she replied. Her expression was taut, as if she expected him to react to the name.

As it happened, he did, but it had nothing to do with Haley's family. The name brought to mind a waiflike creature with pale features and close-cropped hair the color of night. The Ellen he knew was a colleague who had been there for him during a tough time in his life, especially the day his divorce papers came through. He could hardly call it love. More like emotional sustenance. If they hadn't both needed comfort, they might never have progressed past friendship. He frowned, remembering how badly that had turned out.

She had actually accused him of making her pregnant. Until it happened, he would never have dreamed that such a generous woman was capable of such vindictiveness. She had been amazingly persistent, even asked if his protection could have failed. She must have heard that the brand he used had been subject to a recall after a batch was found to be faulty. She probably hoped to take advantage of the product recall to force him into accepting her child as his. It hadn't worked because he had known what Ellen had not, that even without protection, he couldn't give her a child in this lifetime.

He tried to imagine what Haley's Ellen had been like. She had probably been as tawny of coloring as Haley herself, and good-natured enough to make cocoa for him even when she had a problem with him. "I knew an Ellen once," he mused.

Her nerves seemed to stretch to breaking point. "How nice for you."

"It wasn't."

Her eyebrows lifted and her lovely dark eyes met his unwaveringly. Again he had a sense of being accused. But of what? "You didn't have a good relationship?" she asked in a brittle tone.

"It was fine until she lied to me."

"She must have had a good reason."

He felt his frown deepen. Her readiness to side with Ellen, when she didn't know the half of it, fueled his annoyance. "She did. She wanted to trap me into supporting her child."

Droplets of cocoa splashed over the rim of her mug onto the countertop. Her hands were shaking, he noticed. Had he touched a nerve here? Perhaps Joel's father had accused Haley of the same thing.

As she mopped up the spill, she said, "You seem sure it was a trap."

The tremor in her voice told him he was on the right track. She *had* suffered at the hands of Joel's father. Sam found it hard to imagine Haley doing what Ellen had done, lying about who her baby's father was. Her comment proved how foreign the idea was to Haley's nature. "I'm sure," he said heavily. "Believe me, I wish I wasn't."

She looked confused, but he had no intention of explaining, not now, anyway. He might not want to marry her, but he sure as blazes wanted to make love to her, and confessing his inadequacy wouldn't get them off to the start he wanted.

She began to rub her upper arms. "I can turn up the heat if you're cold," he offered. He could think of other ways he could warm her, but didn't think she'd welcome them.

"No need." She drained her mug. "I'll warm up when I get back to bed."

There was a pleasant thought, but he was fairly sure the suggestion didn't include him.

She took her mug to the sink and began to rinse it. "I'll leave first thing in the morning."

He had assumed she would stay, he realized. The prospect had cheered him up as he and his agent worked through the debacle of the tour details. "Do you have to leave?

"You don't need a house sitter if you're staying in town."

At the thought of losing her, a pang shot through

him, the intensity of it catching him by surprise. "I still need my office reorganized," he pointed out.

She paused. "I can do it without living in."

He thought fast. "Won't it be difficult, going backward and forward with the baby and all?"

"I can manage."

"I don't mean to suggest you can't. But why go through the hassle when there's plenty of room here? Unless you feel uncomfortable sharing the house with me. I'll be the soul of propriety." Now why had he said such a fool thing? Around her, propriety was the last thing on his mind.

She seemed to recognize the fact and looked away. "Like you were this afternoon?"

"You didn't want me to kiss you?"

He knew perfectly well that she had, and he read it in her eyes now.

"If I'm going to stay, it mustn't happen again," she said.

Was she talking to herself or to him? He noticed she hadn't said that she didn't *want* it to happen again. A fist closed around his heart. How could he promise anything? In his kitchen, in the middle of the night, she was the most enticing sight he'd seen in a long time.

Every move she made was graceful, even small ones such as the way she dried and replaced the mug in a cupboard. Because of his height, he'd had them built higher than usual, and she had to stretch to reach them. When she did, the robe eased open and her nightdress rode up her long legs. She stood almost on tiptoe, her arm raised over her head like a dancer.

He imagined taking her in his arms and dancing with her right here in the kitchen. Lord, he must be more tired than he thought. Dancing in the kitchen, indeed. He was a writer with a creative mind, but this was getting out of hand. Unfortunately his writer's imagination couldn't come up with a way to stop it. He wasn't entirely sure he wanted to.

"I can't offer any guarantees," he said, choosing his words with care. "I don't think you can, either."

She closed the cupboard door and spun around. He tried to read her expression and saw only confusion. "Next thing, you'll haul out the old chestnut about this being bigger than both of us."

"Are you sure it isn't? Tell me you didn't feel something between us the moment we set eyes on each other?" He hadn't intended to bring this up so soon, but if he didn't, she would run like a rabbit, then he'd never find out what they could be to each other.

She lowered those impossibly long lashes over her chocolate eyes. "I have no idea what you mean?"

"Then I'll have to remind you."

He was across the kitchen in two seconds and had her in his arms in three. The moment he drew her against him, his tiredness melted away, replaced by a vitality that flowed from her lithe body into his.

He waited for her to protest or push him away. He saw in her eyes the wish that she could do both, yet she did neither. Her hands fluttered as if she didn't know what to do with them, then she rested them against his back where they felt just right.

In his arms, she felt every bit as delicate as she looked, but he also felt her core of strength and thought of tigers. He knew she could be one when aroused. The sight of her holding a poker over her head, prepared to do battle with an intruder to defend her child came back to him. Woe betide anyone who threatened her world or those she loved. Not that he had any such intention. He was more interested in finding a way into that world.

She gave a soft sigh that melted his soul and her eyes drifted closed, although her eyelids quivered, as if she fought a mental battle with herself. He kept his eyes open, absorbing every detail of her lovely face so close to him that he smelled the spearmint toothpaste she'd used before retiring. Added to a hint of cocoa, it tugged at his senses as powerfully as the costliest French perfume. He couldn't help himself. He simply had to taste it.

He dipped his head and sampled her lips, heard her breath rush out, tasted the spearmint and chocolate as a fresh, tingling zest against his mouth. Her mouth softened and warmed under his explorations. Everything in him urged him to take without care, to plunge and plunder, until he'd drunk his fill of her feminine sweetness. Afraid of alarming her, he reined in the urge, limiting himself to kissing her more deeply. The response tore through him until he ached with wanting more than a kiss.

He had to stop before he gave in to the urges rampaging through him. She wasn't ready for more yet, but if he had anything to say in the matter, she would be. As he ended the kiss, her eyes opened wide, the irises huge and dark. "Now do you understand?" he asked.

She slid along the cupboards, feeling her way with her hands like a blind person, as if belatedly deciding to put some distance between them. "I understand only too well. You've just given me the best reason to pack up and leave."

"What are you afraid of?" he asked on a sudden impulse.

She pulled herself up and belted the robe more securely around her waist. Regret pierced him as the satin material swamped his view of the tantalizing valley between her breasts. She had felt so soft and inviting pressed against him. It seemed sinful to cover such beauty. "I'm not afraid of you," she denied. "Should I be?"

"Good grief, no. I'd never force myself on you. And I didn't now," he added, when she opened her mouth to protest.

He saw her accept the truth of it. "No, you didn't. All right, I concede there's something between us, but it can't be anything more than chemistry."

Why can't it? he wanted to ask, but sensed that it was too soon. Something had made her man-shy. If he was to overcome it, he'd have to be careful. "Would it help if I promise only to kiss you by invitation next time?"

It was rash, and he wasn't sure he could keep the

promise, but it was the right thing to say, and he saw her tension visibly ease.

"There won't be a next time."

"Then you will stay?"

"It does make sense to stay until the job's done."

"And if the strike is called off, and I have to hit the road again at short notice, it's easier if you're already settled in here." He didn't see the need to add how unlikely it was that the tour would resume anytime soon. No sense in undoing all his good work.

Her brow furrowed as she thought it through. "That's true. And your office does need a lot of work. Very well, I'll stay."

She wanted to stay as much as he wanted her to, he concluded from the ready way she gave in. His mood had taken a battering during the frustrating day, but he felt it lighten. The memory of her mouth against his washed through his mind, heating his blood. Such a tantalizing taste and so filled with promise.

She might dismiss it as chemistry but she wanted him as much as he wanted her. He had been hurt by Christine and the gods that dictated how fertile a man would be. He gathered that Haley had been hurt by Joel's father, so neither of them was likely to want anything lasting. But they could gain something from one another in the short term. If they were lucky, and it was as special and wonderful as he expected, it might be enough for them both. Losing the tour was starting to seem like a gift.

"Then I'll see you in the morning," he said. "I

should warn you, I'm an early riser. I get most of my writing done before the rest of the world is up and about. I'll try not to disturb you.''

"You won't, I sleep like a log,'' she assured him. ''Especially if Joel has me up during the night, although he's sleeping through more often now.''

"It must be hard for you, coping on your own.''

"It is, but we do okay,'' she said. He saw a shutter come down on her expression. What had he said? One of these days he was going to get out of her exactly what had happened between her and Joel's father, then maybe she could start to heal. Until then, she was like a primed fuse. One spark was all it would take to ignite all that pent-up anger and bitterness, he sensed.

Someone as lovely as Haley shouldn't be possessed by anger, he thought, knowing exactly how she should be possessed. Enough of that line of thinking. He had vowed to keep his hands off her until she gave the green light. All he had to do was figure out how to get her to that point before his office was a model of neatness. It wasn't going to happen tonight. ''I'll reset the alarm. You go on back to bed.''

"If you're sure? I am your employee, after all.''

"Not after hours. And I'm not an ogre during working hours either, unless I'm interrupted while I'm writing.'' *Or somebody lied to him,* he thought, but didn't add. He didn't expect it to be a problem with Haley.

She didn't reply and as she left the kitchen, she skirted around him as if she expected him to turn into an ogre in spite of his assurances. He frowned, not liking that one bit. It was one thing to have her resist the attraction between them, and another for her to be afraid of him. He'd give a lot to know who had instilled that fear in her. If he could get his hands on the man who had hurt her, he'd show the cur how to treat a lady.

Sleep was more elusive than ever, Haley found when she returned to bed. She heard Sam pass her door. His footsteps hesitated for a moment and she held her breath, not sure if it was because he might come in, or because she feared he wouldn't.

The breath escaped in a rush as his footsteps continued down the hall. She heard a door open and close, then silence. She told herself she was glad that she didn't have to listen to the small sounds of Sam getting ready for bed, but found her ears straining all the same.

Her body felt overheated and she impatiently pushed the covers aside, letting the cool night air caress her like a touch. It could have been Sam's touch, she thought in shock. At a word of encouragement from her, he would have been sharing this bed with her now, she was certain. She had felt the hunger in him when he kissed her, and had barely stopped herself from answering it with her own.

What was the matter with her? She had let him kiss her not once, but twice, and had enjoyed it both times. This wasn't part of her plan. He had fathered a child by her sister, then rejected both of them—and stolen her sister's idea, to boot. Her anger flared as she recalled how he had accused Ellen of trying to trap him into supporting her child. *Her* child, she noted. Not his or theirs. How could Haley have let him kiss her or imagine sharing his bed after that?

She felt torn between loyalty to her sister's memory and her own desires. This time desire had nearly won, but it wasn't going to happen again. He had said he would only kiss her by invitation, so it was up to her to make sure she issued none. From now on, she vowed, it would be strictly business between them.

Chapter Four

Joel gave a lusty cry from the other room and Haley
tore her attention away from the computer in Sam's
office. Her heart sank. Surely the baby couldn't be
awake so soon? She had put him down for a nap in
his carrier in the library only half an hour ago and
had hoped to get a substantial amount of work done
before he stirred.

"The best-laid plans of mice and mothers," she
murmured, getting up resignedly.

"It isn't your fault that I'm crabby," she said as
she picked up the crying child, her mood lifting the
moment she cradled his warm body against her. His
tears dried like magic. "Blame it on the chaos next
door. Beats me how even The Beast can get anything
done with his office in such a mess. He's well rid of
that former assistant of his, although he was probably

the only person he could find to put up with his grumpy disposition,'' she told the baby.

Joel's head lolled against her shoulder, and he speared his thumb into his mouth. "Mem-mem,'' he said around it.

She sighed, knowing from experience that he hadn't had enough sleep, but also aware that it was futile trying to convince him. They would both pay for it later when tiredness finally overcame him. "Don't you mean 'men'?'' she said with a wry smile. She blew a raspberry against his silken cheek, earning a babyish chuckle. "I keep forgetting that you are one. Or you will be when you grow up. If I have anything to do with it, you'll grow into one of those sensitive new-age paragons women dream about.''

"Somebody mention my name?''

She almost choked as Sam breezed into the room, his arrival setting her senses on instant alert. Nobody in their right mind would call him sensitive or new-age, far less a paragon, she thought, annoyed with herself for reacting so strongly but unable to prevent it. Toward her sister he had been as insensitive as humanly possible. He was being more reasonable toward Haley herself, but only because he needed her help, she assumed.

He had been right when he described himself as a bear when he was working. The previous morning she had made the mistake of trying to ask him something while he was writing. His response had been unprintable. She had expected him to apologize later but was still waiting.

"Let me guess—you used to be conceited, but now you're perfect," she said with exaggerated sweetness.

He favored her with a smile calculated to melt stone. "Of course."

Feeling herself start to respond, she resisted, the child in her arms reminding her that Sam's smile was as superficial as his Mr. Nice Guy image. Nice guys didn't deny their own offspring, or steal other people's ideas and pass them off as their own, she thought.

The warning didn't stop a wave of internal heat racing from the soles of her feet all the way to her ears. She buried her face against Joel so Sam wouldn't see the effect he had on her.

He went to a shelf of reference books and pulled one out, thumbing through it and reading until she heard his murmur of satisfaction. "Thought so, but it's nice to be proven right." He fixed her with a triumphant glare before adding, she would swear for her sake, "As usual."

Since he had installed her in his office Sam had taken to writing on a laptop computer in his study. He had been at his desk when she rose this morning, and had worked right through breakfast. She hadn't minded fending for herself, being accustomed to it in her own home, but she had felt surprisingly lonely eating in Sam's vast dining room with only Joel for company. Sam had a cleaner who came in twice a week, but had informed her that he only employed a cook when he entertained, adding that he preferred not to have staff underfoot all the time. Which made her wonder why he had been so insistent that she live in.

Reminding herself that she was an employee, not a guest, hadn't lessened her feeling of being neglected, unreasonable though she knew she was being. She had told Joel they were better off without Sam, since he was as likely to bite their heads off as to make polite conversation first thing in the morning, but the thought didn't make her feel any better. After only three days of living and working under Sam's roof, she had started to relish the electric atmosphere that charged the air whenever he was around. He was a brilliant conversationalist, moving from subject to subject with fascinating ease. She couldn't remember when she had found a man's company so stimulating. It took an effort to remind herself that electricity was as dangerous as it was elemental.

Now she was curious in spite of herself. "What are you right about this time?"

"The migratory habits of whales." He made a few notes on a scrap of paper that he then tucked into his shirt pocket.

"Yesterday it was pack ice," she commented. "Where's Cosmic Panda off to this time? The Antarctic?"

"He's on an ice-bound planet that has a lot in common with the Antarctic," he confirmed, replacing the book on the shelf. He linked both hands behind his neck and tilted his head back, stretching. "Right now he isn't going anywhere. I'm written out for today. And my agent has been nagging me about the Children's Literature Archive. I promised to loan them the artwork from the first book for an exhibition, and I've put off organizing it until it's become urgent. I was hoping you could apply your efficient mind to the task.''

Here was the opportunity she'd been waiting for. Some of her half sister's work was likely to be among the artwork. Depending on when it was dated, it could give Haley the evidence she needed that Ellen had invented the Cosmic Panda character. Haley subdued the twinge of conscience that followed this thought by reminding herself that she needed the proof for Joel's sake. "I'd be happy to do it."

Sam gestured to the baby in her arms. "Won't you find it difficult, working one-handed?"

She gave him a rueful glance. "I tried to get him to sleep, but Joel has other ideas." As if on cue the baby yawned hugely and scrubbed his eyes with his fist.

"Would it help if I tell him a story?"

She knew Sam was only offering to help so she could take over the task of preparing the artwork for the exhibition, but her spirits lifted anyway. She had been wondering how to get Sam to spend more time with his son. He might not be willing to acknowledge his position, but she was determined that Joel would know his father better than she had known hers. "That's a good idea," she said brightly.

"It means you'll have to deal with the artwork on your own until I can get Joel off to sleep."

"I don't mind. It's what I'm here for." At least as far as Sam was aware.

"I could get used to having your help," he said.

She shook her head. "Not a good idea." Especially not for her peace of mind.

"You don't like the work?"

"I love it, but your office won't always be in chaos. What would I do then?"

"Work for me on other projects. You can see for yourself how much I need a permanent assistant."

"I can hardly deny it, but my answer is still no." Even if she hadn't felt so strongly attracted to Sam, the baby in her arms argued against any chance that she and Sam could work together on a lasting basis.

He lifted his hands shoulder-width apart. "I know I can be hard to get along with at times."

Wincing, she untangled Joel's fingers from the bird's nest he had been making in her hair. "That has to be the understatement of the year. When you snapped at me yesterday morning, I learned a whole new vocabulary."

Sam massaged his chin with one hand. "I warned you what I'm like when I'm working."

"It's true, you did." Pity nobody had warned her about his effect on her as well.

Joel patted her face to retrieve her attention, and she kissed each of his tiny fingers in turn. The baby gurgled in delight, and tried to catch her hand. She had worked for enough difficult bosses to be able to handle one grouchy writer, she told herself. It was simply a process of giving as good as she got, until they accepted that they couldn't treat her like part of the furniture.

Much harder to cope with was the way Sam affected her as a woman. Reminding herself that he was The Beast didn't stop her heart from hammering and her pulse from racing whenever he came within her orbit. "I'm not interested in a full-time job," she said, hating the tremor she heard in her voice.

Sam didn't seem to notice. "Wouldn't it be easier to raise a baby on a reliable income instead of the hit-and-miss consultancy fees you must be living on now?"

She welcomed the anger that flooded through her. "Thanks for the vote of confidence in my ability."

He looked nonplussed. "I wasn't implying any such thing."

"You're only suggesting that I can't take care of myself and my son."

Sam raked his fingers through his hair, leaving trails that Haley was annoyed to find she wanted to smooth away. "I only meant that a regular job would make your task easier. You can't deny that. And you accuse me of having a hair-trigger temper."

"I didn't mean to snap," she said, knowing that he was right about the job. But arguing about it wouldn't change her mind. Worse, his presence was heightening her awareness of him to a degree that made her feel like a human tuning fork. "I guess I'm a little tired."

"Because Joel kept you awake for half the night?" Sam asked.

She knew she looked as contrite as she felt. "I hope we didn't disturb you."

"I'm not worried for myself. From having my sister's babies around, I learned that you can't turn them on and off like machines."

"More's the pity sometimes," she said, her smile at Joel softening the comment. "Other mothers assure me that he won't always be waking up at all hours. They also tell me that he'll progress to crawling at a million miles an hour, terrifying me by trying to climb stairs as soon as he can walk then when he hits two, throwing temper tantrums to bring the house down."

Sam grimaced. "That's supposed to make you feel better?"

"Strangely enough it does. It makes parenthood a constant voyage of discovery, as you'll find out when you try it."

"Not something I'm likely to do."

She had spoken without thinking, completely forgetting for a moment that he had fathered the child in her arms, then declined to make a place for him in his life. "This discussion must be boring you," she said shortly, and turned to place Joel in his carrier. At once the baby began to object at the top of his lungs.

"Here, let me." Sam leaned across her and lifted Joel out again. The novelty of finding himself in masculine arms was enough to silence the baby's yells, and he patted Sam's mouth, evidently finding the rough texture of Sam's skin intriguing, because he kept exploring, hiccuping slightly as his tears dried.

She waited for Sam to object. When he didn't, she said, "You don't have to hold him if you'd rather not. He sometimes cries when I first put him to bed, but he usually settles down after a short time."

"And makes himself miserable in the process. We can't have that, can we, Joel? How about I tell you that story I promised you, while your mother has a break?"

She told herself she had wanted Joel to spend time with his father, but something very like jealousy seared through her. It was all she could do not to snatch her child away from him. "Don't you mean while I organize the artwork for the exhibition?" she said.

Sam's level gaze met hers and he shook his head. "I mean have a break. Take some time off. I'll be fine with Joel while you take an hour or so for yourself. You haven't had any time off since you got here."

"What about the exhibition?"

"They've waited this long. Another day or so won't make much difference."

It was out before she could stop herself. "But you don't like babies."

Sam's scathing look raked her. "Where did you get a fool idea like that?"

Haley could hardly admit it was from the way he had treated her sister when he learned that she was expecting his child, so she said, "Every time I say something about having some of your own, you become cold and distant. I thought—"

"Well, you thought wrong," he said, his tone frigid. "Obviously I wouldn't do the work I do if I didn't like children."

As long as they didn't cramp his lifestyle, Haley surmised. She had friends who freely admitted that they enjoyed having Joel around, provided they could hand him back to her at the end of a visit. Sam might feel the same way. He certainly hadn't reacted to the idea of fatherhood with anything like delight.

The thought of how he *had* reacted was enough to chill her to the bone. "Thanks for offering to mind Joel, but it's best if I look after him myself." She went to take the baby from him. "Baby-sitting is hardly the boss's job."

"Then you agree I'm your boss," he said, not relinquishing his hold on Joel.

She let her wary gaze settle on the two of them, disturbed by the likeness she saw between them. "For the moment."

"Then as your boss, I'm ordering you to get some rest. We both are, aren't we, Joel?"

Sam picked up a cat-shaped crystal paperweight from a shelf and held it up to the light in front of Joel. Fascinated, the baby watched the play of sunshine through it, then reached for the bauble. "Beb-me-beb."

Sam nodded as if he understood perfectly. "You see? Joel agrees with me."

"Two against one is hardly fair."

"Then you agree you're outvoted?"

Since the alternative was to make a scene that

could upset Joel, she decided to give in for the moment. "Very well, I'll go. But call me if you—if he—needs anything."

"It's a promise." He waited until she moved reluctantly toward the door before asking, "How will you spend your free time?"

"Probably worrying," she said over her shoulder.

As she flounced out of the room she knew she needn't worry that Joel would be all right with Sam. She had seen enough to know he could take care of a baby. Evidently his sister had taught him well. Haley was ashamed to admit to herself that she was more worried on her own account. She didn't like the way she had begun to feel around Sam, as if he was less The Beast of her sister's experience and more a man she could care about if she let herself.

On reaching her room she realized she hadn't a clue how to spend the time off Sam had given her. Long before she met Sam she had become so used to working while Joel napped, devoting all her time to him when he was awake, that the idea of an uninterrupted hour to herself was an unaccustomed luxury.

A bath, she thought in sudden inspiration. An en suite bathroom opened off her room and was equipped with a marble hot tub. She had eyed it covetously since she arrived without any real hope that she would have the time to enjoy it.

Guiltily she thought of the artwork waiting to be catalogued for the exhibition. She should get on with it not only because it was part of the work Sam was paying her to do, but also for the chance to find proof that Cosmic Panda was her half sister's creation.

Suddenly an echo of her sister's voice ran through her mind. "Lighten up, Haley. Life is short. Why don't you learn to enjoy it?"

Life was indeed short, Haley thought. Who knew that better than she did? She quieted her conscience, and began to get ready for her bath.

"Wonder what your mommy's doing with her free time," Sam said as he settled the baby on the sofa beside him amid a bank of cushions. "Probably working. Did you know your mother's in danger of becoming a workaholic?"

Joel murmured as if in agreement and Sam felt something tighten deep inside him. Maybe this wasn't a good idea after all. His sister often co-opted him to help bathe or read to his niece and nephew on his frequent visits to their house, but rarely was he entirely alone with them for more than short periods. Since learning that he would never father a child of his own, he had avoided being alone with Jessie's two, he acknowledged to himself. Dearly though he loved them, they reminded him too strongly that this was as close as he would ever come to fatherhood.

From a desk drawer in his office he retrieved a manuscript of a book he'd been working on between other projects. Sam had commissioned an artist to draw some multicolored animals to accompany his nonsense rhyme about a painted zoo where everything was new, zebras were blue and gnus were, too.

"You're the first reader to see this," he told Joel. "So I'd like some noises of appreciation or else I won't have the nerve to give it to my agent. She's expecting another Panda book, and you know how agents are about clients going off in risky new directions. No, you wouldn't know, would you? Maybe you will one day, if you take after your mother in the brains department. Looks, too. Man to man, don't you agree she's gorgeous?" Joel made an impatient sound, and pawed at the book. Sam smiled, getting the message. "Okay, here goes."

As he read aloud Sam exaggerated the words, making the baby laugh by stretching out the mooing sounds as he read about blue kangaroos and a spruce puce goose. Part of Sam's mind drifted to Haley and what she might be doing. He hoped she wasn't working. Her lovely eyes were already shadowed from lack of sleep. She wouldn't be much use to him if she killed herself with work and worry about Joel.

At the same time Sam knew he was mainly worried about Haley herself, rather than her usefulness to him. When had he started caring so much? He had carefully cultivated a reputation as a slave driver of an employer because it got results while saving him from getting involved in his employees' private lives. So his feelings toward Haley were out of character.

She was different. She didn't feel like hired help. She felt more as if—he searched his mind for the right concept—as if she was at home here. As if she belonged. Joel felt as if he belonged here, too, in a way Sam couldn't quite pin down. He had felt a bond with the baby from the moment Haley had forced him to acknowledge Joel's existence on his front doorstep.

"It's because you're such a picture-perfect baby," he told Joel, but knew there was more. Sam's puzzling feeling of connection with the baby didn't lessen even when Joel was screaming his head off to let them know it was time he was changed.

Sam told himself that having a baby under his roof was the last thing he should want. Was he a glutton for punishment, or was there something special about Joel himself?

He looked down at the baby's golden head bent over the colorful pages of the manuscript. "Yeah, you're pretty special," Sam said gruffly. Maybe the father thing was what they had in common. Sam had grown up without his dad, and Joel was about to do the same. It might explain why Sam felt so connected to the baby.

Joel grabbed a handful of page. "Da-da."

As Sam untangled the paper from the baby's hand, he felt a pang at the sight of the tiny fingers curling around his own. "I've been called a lot of names in my time, but I'm afraid daddy isn't going to be one of them," he said. "Believe me, I know what it's like to grow up without your father. Mine died when I was nine, but at least I had the chance to know him and we had some great times together. You won't even have that."

Sam's voice became hoarse, and he coughed to clear it, caught off guard as memories of times spent with his father flooded him. He couldn't remember back to when he'd been Joel's age, but he could remember when he wasn't much older, riding on a painted black pony on a carousel in downtown Canberra with his father holding on to the saddle so Sam would feel secure.

The carousel was still there, and Sam wondered how it would feel to stand alongside Joel while he rode the same black horse. It wasn't going to happen, he told himself, blinking hard. Haley had her own agenda for her son, and had made it obvious that her plans didn't include a man in her life.

He wasn't going to let one small baby and his beautiful mother get to him, Sam told himself resolutely. "Look, here's a teal seal and a pea-green eel, drinking juice with the spruce puce goose," he read aloud, showing the pictures to Joel and trying not to wonder what Haley was doing right now.

Up to her neck in fragrant bubbles, Haley was having a much harder time relaxing than she thought she should. The water was warm and she had set the spa jets to a turbulence that massaged without buffeting her too much. Her head rested against a bath pillow and through a picture window alongside the tub, she had a view of Sam's garden all the way to the lake through the one-way glass. At least she hoped it was one-way. Not that Sam would be interested in her even if he did chance to walk past the window, but there was no point playing with fire. He was a man, after all.

He was certainly that, she mused. The description

"alpha male" fitted him perfectly. Pity his super-charged testosterone levels had to include such beastly grumpiness. No, it was a good thing. Someone as attractive as Sam would be almost impossible to resist when he turned on the charm.

Not that it would change her opinion of him, she assured herself, adjusting the jets to a more comfort-able setting. Her interest in Sam was purely on Joel's behalf. All right, she had slipped a bit when she let Sam kiss her. Maybe she had even enjoyed it. A lot. But there would be no repeats.

With an angry twist of her hand, she turned the jets off and climbed out of the water. What was she doing mooning about kissing Sam when she had work to do? She swathed a bath sheet around herself and wrapped another around her hair. Sam had handed her the perfect opportunity to do a little sleuthing on Joel's behalf while he was minding the baby. She would never have a better chance to prove once and for all that Sam was The Beast of her sister's expe-rience.

Chapter Five

The sound of a hairdryer buzzing led Sam to the bathroom off Haley's bedroom. The door stood open. He started to knock on the frame, then let his hand drop, mesmerized by the sight of her swathed in a bath sheet, her legs and feet bare. Her slender arms were upraised as she pulled a long-toothed comb through her hair with one hand, aiming the dryer with the other. The sight of her glowing skin and graceful movements made him swallow hard. When she hadn't answered his knock, he should have had the sense to come back later instead of venturing into no-man's land.

Why had he done it? He was curious, he admitted to himself. The time he had just spent with her child made him want to be closer to Haley. Who was she, really? Not the superficial details such as where she lived and what she did for a living, but who was she deep down? He wanted to know what she loved and hated, what made her laugh and cry, what tastes made her close her eyes in ecstasy. How he could make her react the same way to him.

This thought brought him up short. Being around the baby must be making him soft, he decided. His life was already complicated enough without adding Haley and her child to the mix. And he sensed that if he did, it wouldn't stop at a love-'em-and-leave-'em affair. She didn't strike him as the type. Certifiably crazy, he told himself. Get out now, while you still can.

He stayed where he was.

He sniffed the air, scenting bath lotion, and noticed a rim of foam clinging to the tub. He felt the corners of his mouth tug upward. So that was how she had spent her time. Pity he'd been otherwise engaged. The tub was plenty big enough for two.

Annoyed with himself for being so fanciful, he frowned.

She looked up and saw him. He was gratified to see a blush start before she concealed it behind an angry glare as she turned the dryer off. In the sudden well of silence her breathing sounded labored. "Don't you know it's polite to knock?"

"I did, twice. You didn't hear me over that thing."

She aimed the dryer at him like a pistol. "Did you want something?"

"Not a good question to ask a man when all you're wearing is a towel."

That got to her, he saw, watching more color spread like brushfire across her beautiful features. He saw her struggle with herself as if she didn't know whether to feel complimented or offended. Too bad offended won.

"A gentleman wouldn't barge into a lady's bathroom. If he had to, he'd avert his eyes," she snapped.

Obviously she didn't realize what a waste that would be. "I never claimed to be a gentleman," he said evenly. "Anyway that towel covers more than most bathing suits. I only wanted to tell you that I got Joel to sleep so you can take as long as you like."

"You left him alone?"

Her anger aroused his own. He might have been short-changed in the baby-making department, but he had more sense than that. "Relax, will you? I've plugged in a baby monitor beside his carrier. My sister uses it when she brings the children to visit. I've put the receiver in your bedroom for now and you can move it wherever you want to. You'll be able to hear the moment Joel wakes up."

Lowering the dryer she realized she'd been hefting like a weapon, Haley felt her anger subside, leaving a prickly feeling of awareness that could only come from Sam himself. She made herself resist it. Strictly business, remember? It was hard to keep in mind when he affected her so strongly. Too bad it was one-sided, she thought, remembering the frown on his face as he'd watched her. "In that case, as soon as I'm dressed we can get started organizing the artwork," she said coolly as she could.

He nodded as if welcoming the switch to more practical matters. "I've put the files in my office so you can be close by for Joel."

He left and she told herself she must have imagined the fire in his eyes when she looked up and saw him in the doorway. Her heart began to race from the bath no doubt. If he'd felt anything at the sight of her clad only in a towel, he'd done a good job of concealing it. He'd sounded angry, probably because she was taking more time away from the job than he'd wanted her to.

By the time she was dressed in a pair of wide-legged navy pants and a white shell slashed with red lightning bolts, her hair swept into a high ponytail, she had worked herself into a temper to match Sam's. He was the one who'd insisted she take some time off. Let him so much as criticize her and she'd let him have it with both barrels.

He seemed to sense her mood as soon as she joined him in the office. He was sorting through a pile of original artwork. Her heart began to pound, but she saw at a glance that none of the work was done in her half sister's distinctive style. All of these sketches must be from the first book rather than from the early development of the Cosmic Panda character, the sketches Haley most wanted to locate.

He gestured to a sheet of paper on the letterhead of the Children's Literature Archive. "Everything they need is spelled out here. They don't want only the final artwork but also the rough sketches that show how the character came into being."

So did she, Haley thought, feeling her heart pick up speed again. "This is all finished art," she pointed out.

"I thought we'd start here before progressing to the other files," he said. "Since my old assistant left, I'm not sure where anything is any more."

"So I gather from the state of your office."

"What's got into you?" he demanded. "A hot tub is supposed to relax you, not put a bee in your bonnet.

She was disappointed, she recognized. Not only because Sam had seemed indifferent to her in the bathroom. That was what she wanted, wasn't it? But because he hadn't reacted more favorably to spending time with Joel.

Well, what had she expected? He hadn't welcomed the baby with open arms when Ellen had told him she was pregnant. So why was Haley surprised that he didn't melt over Joel now?

"How did you like baby-sitting?" she asked, pushing him.

With his hands full of drawings he tensed. "It's hardly my first time."

"How old are your sister's children?"

He thought for a moment. "Jason is seven months, and Laurel is two."

"And their father?"

"A bit absent-minded, but devoted to them and my sister."

For a second, Sam sounded wistful, she thought. It prompted her to ask, "Did you have a good relationship with your father?"

"For as long as it lasted."

She felt her eyebrow lift and wondered if she'd stumbled on a clue to Sam's rejection of Joel. "Did he leave your family?"

"He died when I was nine."

Because she didn't know what to say, she reached past Sam and picked up several of the drawings. The gesture brought her arm into contact with his, and the slight brush was enough to make sparks flash inside her, as if she'd touched a live electric wire. He frowned, aware of the movement, although hardly of the reason for it. "It isn't contagious. He had cancer."

Since she didn't want to explain that Sam himself was the reason for her reaction, she drew her mouth into a line. "You don't have to talk about it if you'd rather not."

"There's nothing to talk about." He sounded unruffled, but she was alert enough to his mood to detect an undercurrent of something more. Resentment? She knew how that felt. As a child, she had wasted a lot of time being angry at her father for deserting her. At least she'd had the hope that he might one day come back, but in Sam's case, his father's death had offered no such hope.

"I grew up without my dad," she said, not sure why she felt moved to share the information with him. "But leaving was his decision."

"Tough call."

"Not as tough as yours."

Sam's hands stilled on a large color picture of what appeared to be a draft of a book cover. He stared at it as if hardly seeing it. "I could handle losing him," he said in a tone like ice. "What I couldn't handle was the way my mother lied to me over it. Instead of telling me he was tired and needed rest, she should have come out and told me he was dying."

"She probably wanted to protect you." As a mother herself, Haley understood the desire.

He nodded. "No doubt but she denied me the chance to say everything I wanted to say to my dad, to store up memories for when he wasn't around. The truth may be hard to take, but lies only make matters worse."

The vehemence Haley heard in his voice made her squirm inwardly. How would Sam react if he knew Haley had also lied to him? Like his mother, Haley had good reason, but he wouldn't necessarily agree. Haley knew she shouldn't care. He was The Beast and had treated her sister and his baby abominably. But even beasts had feelings, as he'd just shown.

Haley was surprised at the depth of compassion he had aroused in her. She knew no matter how she justified deceiving him she couldn't make herself feel good about it. What he'd revealed had only made her feel more wretched.

At a squawk coming through the baby monitor's receiver, she started to get up but Sam said, "I'll go."

"I'll come, too. He probably needs changing by now."

"And you think I can't cope?"

The edge was back in his voice, the fleeting moment of revelation at an end, she gathered. "Be my guest," she ground out.

At the door he caught her arm and swung her around to face him. "Whatever hassles you may have had with Joel's father, take my advice and get over them."

She stared at him, achingly aware that the sudden closeness had set her senses singing. She took refuge in anger. "What?"

"Even if you can't stand the sight of him, he has the right to get to know his child, for Joel's sake."

Iced water ran down her spine. Sam had no idea what he was saying. "This is hardly your concern," she said furiously, the irony slamming home to her.

He didn't relinquish his hold and his eyes flashed flame. "We both lost our fathers for different reasons so we know the hole it leaves in your life. You have a good kid there. Don't put him through the same hell."

She drew herself up. "When you're prepared to take responsibility for a child, you'll have the right to dictate parenting methods to me, not before."

He pulled her against him. His body felt like iron. "What the blazes is that supposed to mean?"

She had already said too much. "Take it any way you like."

He looked as if he wanted to break something, quite possibly her. Instead his mouth descended on hers in a kiss that felt like a flash flood, washing away everything but awareness of the moment. Her mind spun out of control.

He had promised not to kiss her again until she asked him to, and nothing in their conversation had amounted to an invitation, she thought with the fragment of her mind still capable of coherent thought. She was furious with him, and with herself for responding when she knew she should push him away. Yet she found herself clinging to him as the room spun around her.

It was just as well that Joel's cries began to escalate. Sam let her go, looking almost as thunderstruck as she felt. Shakily she walked into the library and picked the baby up, finding him as damp as she'd expected. She carried him into the bedroom where she assembled what she needed. Her hands trembled as she changed him.

Sam followed them, his expression dark as he observed the process. When she finished, he lifted Joel from her arms, and she watched a sea change come over his face. "Better now?" he asked the baby.

Joel's baby chatter in reply made her frown. She was still seething from Sam's presumption that she was selfishly keeping her child from his father, when nothing could be further from the truth. "How come you get the good part, leaving me with the cleaning up?" she demanded.

Sam swung the baby high into the air, earning a squeal of delight. "You can't say I didn't offer. But to prove I was sincere, why don't I take Joel out for some fresh air to give you a clear shot with the artwork?"

"You're all heart."

He dropped into a chair and sat Joel on his knee. "I meant what I said about Joel knowing his dad. No matter what's between the two of you, it's the right thing to do. But I was out of line in the way I brought it up."

"Apology accepted," she said, although what he'd said hardly qualified as one.

He bumped Joel up and down on his knee. "Glad we got that straightened out."

If Sam expected her to admit that she'd also spoken out of turn, he was in for a long wait, she thought. Sam obviously enjoyed the baby's company. But when it came to taking responsibility for Joel, Sam had a long way to go.

Chapter Six

A couple of days later, Sam appeared at the office door. He watched her for a moment before saying, "Come outside. It's too nice a day to be working. You and Joel could use the fresh air."

She kept her gaze on the monitor screen for fear of betraying how tempted she was to accept. Since the moment he had turned into The Beast her sister had known, accusing Haley of keeping Joel away from his father for her own selfish reasons, she had tried to keep her promise to maintain a businesslike relationship with Sam.

He wasn't making it easy. As well as taking turns cooking dinner, he had started bringing her coffee and fresh muffins at the desk, and had volunteered to play with Joel while she worked. It was becoming harder to reconcile the way he acted now with the man who had betrayed Ellen.

For someone who hadn't wanted to know about his child, he was prepared to give Joel a lot of attention, Haley thought. Did Sam somehow sense the blood tie that bound them, responding to it in spite of his reluctance to admit paternity?

She had been bathing the baby in the bathtub yesterday when Sam had propped himself against the wall to watch. She had surprised a silly grin on his face, and tartly suggested he lend a hand. He had supported the slippery baby like an expert, cooing nonsense words to Joel while she got a towel ready.

He hadn't objected when Joel splashed an obviously expensive shirt with soapy water. In fact, he had seemed to enjoy himself. Haley's pulse picked up speed as she remembered the way the wet shirt had defined his superb musculature. When she took the baby from him, Sam's hand had trailed over her arm, sending a shiver through her. She had told herself she was simply chilled, but meeting his warm gaze had exposed the lie.

She didn't want this, she told herself urgently. Wanting him was one thing, a biological urge that she couldn't control. But she could control what she did about it. She shook her head. "I have to finish this."

He rested a hand on her shoulder. "You've already done more in a week than I expected in a month. Look at this place."

She didn't need to look. She was well aware of the difference she'd made in his office. The piles of old reference materials had been sorted, and the useful cuttings filed where they could do him some good. When she finished, he would be able to locate anything he needed at a moment's notice.

Unfortunately, the work had also kept her from going through the files of old artwork that might have given her the proof she sought that Cosmic Panda had been her sister's creation. To Haley's frustration, Sam had decided to get the artwork ready for the exhibition by himself, thinking he was doing her a favor. She could hardly object without betraying her secret agenda.

Sam's computer was the last remaining hurdle, and she was busy reorganizing the contents into files and folders instead of the present confusion. She'd spent most of yesterday backing up work-in-progress for him. She winced, thinking of his laissez-faire attitude to saving work. One of these days he'd lose something he couldn't replace.

When she said so, he merely shrugged. "I back up manuscripts. The rest are only ideas. Most don't bear fruit anyway."

One of these days they would, she had warned him. So now there were red disks for manuscripts, blue for ideas, yellow for backups. They sat in soldierly rows on a shelf above the desk. She didn't expect him to keep them that way for long, but she wouldn't be around to see what he did with them, so it hardly mattered.

The thought gave her an unexpected jolt, but she dismissed it as a hunger pang. She hadn't thought about taking a break until Sam suggested it. "Any news about the book tour?'' she asked him over her shoulder as her fingers continued to fly over the keys.

He shook his head. ''We might not go ahead with it at all. I can do radio and television interviews from here, and the publicist is setting up a series of Internet chat sessions to let the kids talk to me via the computer. It means the tour, if you can still call it one, can extend all over the world. A new approach for a new century. This strike may have done more good than I expected.''

So he wouldn't need a house sitter, after all. She screened the disappointment out of her tone. ''You can hardly sign books over a computer.''

He flexed his hand. ''I've signed boxloads of copies in the warehouse, ready for when the strike is resolved and they get out to the stores.''

So that's where he had disappeared to yesterday. He had said he was with his publicist, Lori Drake, making Haley wonder if there was more to the relationship than business. Haley had been annoyed to find the possibility bothering her and it infused her voice now. ''Sounds like you've thought of everything.''

He raised a dark eyebrow. ''As a computer person, I thought you'd find the Internet tour concept exciting.''

''I do, of course.'' If it hadn't meant he would have no further need of her.

He folded his arms over his broad chest. ''But?''

She forced a smile. ''No buts. It sounds brilliant.'' Like most things Sam did, she thought. She had seen enough of his work-in-progress to be impressed by his commitment. No word was allowed to remain in a manuscript if he could find a better one. He researched his backgrounds meticulously, then interpreted them in words his young readers could understand, stretching their abilities just enough so they found his books exciting and challenging.

She had to keep reminding herself of her mission to prove that he had stolen her sister's idea, although she had found no evidence so far. As with his behavior toward Joel, her lack of progress only made her feel more confused.

"What about a picnic by the lake?" he suggested.

She felt panic rise, and not only because time was running out. She didn't want to enjoy his company too much. "I told you, I can't." Some demon made her add, "I'm sure Lori wouldn't mind going on a picnic with you."

He pried her hands off the keyboard and held them as he urged her to her feet. Wildfire tore through her and she jerked away as he said, "I'm not asking Lori, I'm asking you. Besides, Joel needs the outing. He's fretful today."

She felt a rush of guilt for working while the baby suffered, although she had already done all she could for him. "He's cutting his first tooth."

"That explains why he's chewing on everything he can get his hands on."

"I gave him some teething medicine this morning and he seemed better."

"He *is* okay, just a bit fractious, so lose the stricken

look, will you? I've seen it on my sister's face a million times and like her, you're a great mother with nothing to feel guilty about. See for yourself.''

She glanced through the open door and saw the baby playing with a ring of plastic keys on a blanket on the floor. After finishing his early morning writing session and a workout in his private gym, Sam had again suggested that he mind Joel while she took over his office. She had resisted at first, thinking he was only offering out of politeness. Seeing them together, she had changed her opinion. He was a natural with children.

It should have been obvious from his choice of work, but the reality was another matter. He seemed to know instinctively how to relate to the baby, and to delight in Joel's gurgling responses.

She couldn't help contrasting Sam's easy relationship with the baby with her own father's discomfort around her. Jealous? she asked herself. No doubt. But she was also puzzled. Sam liked children. He was good with them. So why had he been so angry when Ellen suggested he was the father of her child? Haley could hardly ask him outright, but the question nagged at her.

She bit her lip. It *was* a beautiful day and the fresh air would be good for Joel. Good for her, too. She'd spent far too much time indoors lately.

She arched her back and rolled her head from side to side, working out some of the tension. ''All right, for a little while.''

He gave a satisfied grin. "While you're getting Joel ready, I'll throw together some picnic food."

Later, after an hour relaxing in the shade of a white painted gazebo, eating barbecued chicken with her fingers and watching the ducks play on the lake, she was glad she'd let him talk her into this.

Joel enjoyed kicking his bare legs in the fresh air and sunshine, although his new tooth was obviously bothering him. She was relieved when the baby fell asleep and she settled him in his baby carrier, covering him gently. With both tiny fists curled around the edge of his bunny rug, he looked like an angel.

"Why not take a nap yourself?" Sam suggested, watching her. "You can't keep going without rest."

She shrugged. "I don't have much choice at present."

"There's always a choice."

Reminded of the one he had made in rejecting her sister and the baby, Haley felt her emotions freeze into a hard lump inside her. "Are you saying I shouldn't take care of Joel on my own?" It had never occurred to her to hand him over to anyone else.

Sam shook his head. "I'm not suggesting any such thing. But you don't have to do it alone. I know I asked before, but what about Joel's father?"

Bitterness flooded through her. "He doesn't want to know."

"There are laws forcing him to take responsibility."

"Laws aren't much good if the man denies the baby's his in the first place."

Sam's face took on a strange cast. If she hadn't known better, she would have thought he was angry for her sake. What was going on here? Unless he had one rule for himself, and another for other men. "You shouldn't give up so easily," he advised.

She searched his face, but found only sincerity. "I haven't given up," she assured him in a brittle tone. "I have my own plan for taking care of Sam's father."

"I'm glad to hear it."

He wouldn't be, if he knew what it was. She couldn't help asking, "Why do you care?"

He rolled onto his side and propped himself up on an elbow, his face only inches from hers. "Do you have to ask?"

His breath washed over her like a caress. She felt at risk of drowning in his fluid gaze. "You only met me a couple of weeks ago."

"When you're attracted to someone, it only takes an hour, sometimes only a second for that awareness to flash between you. You can't pretend you don't feel it."

She couldn't because it was true, and she saw him absorb the fact from her expression. He was a writer, words were his stock-in-trade, she reminded herself. It didn't stop her heart from picking up speed and her face from flooding with betraying color. "Even if I had felt it, I still have Joel to consider."

"Surely any man who loves you will also love your son?"

He couldn't mean himself, she thought, hearing the blood roar in her ears. "It's not that simple."

"I'll show you how simple it is." And he reached for her, pulling her against him on the blanket.

The breath trembled through her. When he traced a finger along her jaw, she burned inside. He was right. She had known she wanted him from first meeting, but had fought it, knowing the kind of man he was. In his arms, she was losing the battle, but she had to try. She turned her face away from his although everything in her craved the feel of his mouth against hers. "I can't."

His gaze flickered to Joel and back to her face. "Why not? It's not as if it would be the first time."

"More than you know."

Astonishment, then anger, blazed in his eyes as he reached his own conclusion. "Are you suggesting that Joel's father forced himself on you? It would explain why your response to me is so unworldly, although you've had a child."

She felt her eyes brim and blinked hard to clear them. "It wasn't like that."

He cupped the side of her face so gently that she had to fight the urge to nestle against his hand. "You don't have to tell me any more until you're ready. I just want you to know it doesn't have to be like that. When you both feel the same, it's wonderful and special."

She already felt wonder at the way he made her burn with a touch. No one had ever had such an effect on her before. She felt light as air, capable of soaring with him anywhere he chose to take her.

She didn't protest when he undid the top of her cotton shirt, and slid his hand inside. His eyes darkened as his fingers molded the pliant mounds beneath her shirt. He slipped the garment off her shoulders and bent to worship her breasts with his mouth.

Desire arrowed straight to her heart. She glanced at the lake in consternation. "We can't, not here."

He sensed that her concern wasn't solely for who might see them. "It's okay, the bushes screen us from view. But if you want, we can go back to the house."

She let her head drop back. Her breath became labored as he traced kisses from her breasts all the way up her throat, claiming her mouth like a prize as he reached it. When he drew away, he said, "On the other hand, we might not."

She couldn't have moved to save her life. "It is beautiful here."

"Beautiful." She saw flame in his gaze. "You know I want you, Haley."

"Yes."

"I need to hear you say you want me, too."

He was making sure she didn't repeat what he thought had happened with Joel's father, she understood. She should tell him the truth and end this, but she knew she would have more chance of stopping the breeze from blowing.

His caresses made her feel more beautiful and desirable than she had in a long time. After she took on Joel's care, the only man she had allowed into her life had treated her as if she had ceased being a woman, especially when she refused to let him make love to her. Only as Sam swept her breath away with his touch did she realize she had been at risk of believing it herself. Until now.

He made her feel all woman, all wanton, and she didn't want it, not from him. But as his touch turned from quest into invitation, she couldn't hold back a gasp of pure pleasure. Her pulse hammered and her skin heated. How could she feel hot and shivering all at once? She found herself wishing that Joel would cry, demanding her attention. But the baby slept peacefully, giving her no easy escape.

Why should she resist? She had come for revenge. Surely this would be the sweetest of all, to take what Sam offered, enjoy the satisfaction her soul craved, then abandon him as he had done her sister?

Somehow she knew it wasn't the reason. She nodded. "I want you, too," she said, the words struggling out of a throat made arid by desire.

Sam had known what her answer had to be, but hadn't been sure she would admit it. Her response drove his own desire off the scale. He had never wanted a woman as much as he did Haley. With her mix of innocence and maternal beauty, she had bewitched him from first encounter. He was sure she felt the same, although she resisted it.

If Joel's father had forced himself on her, it would explain a lot. Anger flared through Sam at the thought of someone hurting her. Both his father and stepfather had hammered home the importance of respecting women. Even marriage didn't give a man the right to take whatever he wanted.

It didn't stop him wanting to.

Sam felt the primitive urge driving him right now, but he would no more indulge it without invitation than he would fly. In his book, no meant no. Getting a green light from Haley so soon was a gift he hadn't expected to receive. Hoped for, certainly. Dreamed about, definitely. He wondered if she suspected that spending hours in a warehouse signing books was his equivalent of taking a cold shower.

He reminded himself to go slowly. She had been hurt, and he wanted to show her how different it could be with the right man.

Her skin felt like satin, her hair like a banner of silk as he undid the pins holding it away from her face. He was fascinated by the way the sunlight glinted off it, turning it copper-gold. As his fingers brushed her scalp, he felt her shiver with pleasure, and she closed her eyes.

Cradled in the crook of his arm, she weighed so little. He made a mental note to bring more muffins on her breaks. He knew she wasn't still feeding Joel herself. He hadn't seen her do it, but it didn't stop him wanting to.

At the thought of her with the baby at her breast, his throat closed. Unable to resist, he lowered his head and took one roseate peak in his mouth, hearing her sharply indrawn breath before she clasped her hands to his head, holding him closer. She tasted of sunshine and smelled of gardenias, and his insides clenched so fiercely that he wondered how he was going to honor his vow not to rush this.

As he nuzzled her breast, her hands tangled in his hair. Switching sides, he drew lazy spirals around her other nipple with his tongue. She moaned out loud, her fingers digging into his scalp until waves of sensation surged down his neck and spine.

Slowly, slowly, he reminded himself, but had to lift his head or the battle would be lost. Her heavy-lidded gaze met his. "What are you doing?" she asked.

"Sampling what Joel tasted," he said.

Shock registered in her dark gaze and magenta suffused her features as light dawned. "What? Oh, but I didn't...I mean I'm not... "

He touched a finger to her lips. "I know. I was only curious. You're entitled to make your own choices." He pushed away a faint disappointment. Feeding Joel from a bottle didn't make her less womanly. That was a male fantasy he had no right to force on her.

But his comment troubled her, and he saw fear invade her gaze. He hated himself for putting it there. He had meant to be more careful. They barely knew each other, and already he was so hungry for her that he could hardly think straight.

He felt her grow tense and knew the moment when they might have gone further was over. He didn't try to hold her when she moved away and began to button her blouse. Her fingers were shaking.

"I'm sorry, Sam," she said in a husky voice.

He shook his head and forced himself to sound

reasonable, although he felt anything but. "Nothing to apologize for. There's always next time."

"There won't be a next time," she said fiercely. "Because I won't be here."

Shock speared through him so sharply, he felt it deep in his gut. He swung himself upright. What had he said or done to throw her into such a panic? "You can't go. This is only the beginning."

The fierce shake of her head made her glorious hair swirl around her head. "I only work for you. In another day or so, I'll be finished. There can't be anything else."

He remembered the taste and feel of her, and swallowed hard. "What's between us is real. You can't make it disappear just by wishing."

He bit back any more admissions. He wanted her, sure. He craved the pleasure they could give each other. But he'd learned enough from his short-lived marriage not to risk anything deeper.

Haley had been hurt, too, so he understood if she didn't want commitment, either. Didn't it make them perfect for each other? Obviously, she didn't think so.

She stared at him as if she had heard the words he'd stopped himself from saying. "This wasn't supposed to happen."

He began to pack up the picnic things as a way of avoiding her eyes. If he looked at her, he would have to kiss her again and he wasn't sure he could stop at a kiss. "Lots of things happen that aren't planned."

Like a baby, Haley thought, watching Sam fold the picnic blanket. Her gaze flickered to the carrier where

Joel slept, his thumb anchored in his mouth. Pain fisted around her heart. How could she feel so attracted to the man who had rejected her baby? She only knew she did, and Sam was right, she couldn't wish it away.

She felt angry at herself as wetness stained her cheeks. Sam turned and saw it, too. With a groan, he threw the blanket aside and swept her into his arms. "Tears, Haley? Did I do something?"

In spite of everything, his arms felt so good around her that her tears evaporated. She sniffed. "You didn't do anything. It's me, all me."

His smile broadened. "Let me show you how wrong you are."

He stood up and slid an arm under her legs, sweeping her up so she was forced to link her arms around his neck for balance. She tried to protest, but the pleasure of being in his arms silenced her protestations.

It was good to be held so strongly, to feel beautiful and desirable as he rained kisses on her upturned face. Too often lately, she had wondered if any man would ever desire her again. Why did Sam have to be the one?

He placed her on a bench within the shelter of the gazebo, then went back and brought the baby carrier into the shelter with them. Joel didn't stir. Returning to Haley, Sam placed a cushion under her head, then eased himself down beside her and began to kiss her deeply.

She knew that a word from her was all it would take to make him stop, but the word lodged in her throat. She should say it, but she didn't. What did that make her?

A woman in love, she acknowledged with a feeling of surrender. Sam was the last man she should love, but somewhere between first meeting and his passionate kisses now, it had happened in spite of her best intentions.

His urgent fingers dealt with her clothes. Desire, hot and sweet, raced through her and she arched toward him, clasping her arms around him to bring him closer. Still, it wasn't close enough.

He tore his mouth from hers and lifted his head, his eyes blazing. "Now what was that about leaving?"

The taste of him fogged her senses. "I won't leave," she said, knowing it would have been more honest to say, "I can't."

The gleam of triumph in his eyes showed he'd heard it, anyway. "Do you want me?"

"Yes." There was no other possible answer to that, either.

He made a sound that was half moan and half growl as he undid her jeans to caress her more fully, causing the breath to catch in her throat. With an impatient gasp, she kicked the jeans off altogether, held in thrall by his fiery gaze that never left her face.

Needing to touch him, too, she peeled off his shirt, the sheer magnificence of his body filling her with awe. She let her fingers trail over him. The hardness of his muscles beneath the taut skin made his gentleness all the more awesome.

It was costing him, she discovered as she felt his heart hammer beneath her palm. The only time she had felt this much leashed power was when she had patted a thoroughbred for luck a few minutes before a race. In Sam, she felt a similar strength barely held in check. Her pulse picked up speed as she imagined where such strength might carry them both.

He sat up long enough to kick off his jeans, before gathering her close. It was her heart's turn to leap. When conscience threatened to intervene, she resisted it. That she was behaving as thoughtlessly as Sam himself had done, Haley didn't want to think. Why shouldn't she take what he wanted to give, and she wanted so badly to receive? There would be no consequences. Haley believed in protecting herself, though she hadn't the need so far. After all, wasn't she the orderly one?

Not so orderly now, Haley thought. Desires, needs, sensations whirled through her until she was mindless with them. As his mouth claimed hers, she felt power, danger, and gentleness, all in one long, searing kiss.

She indulged herself by giving in to the urge to caress him. His skin felt fiery but smooth as glass, the angles and planes in wondrous contrast to her own soft curves. She could hardly believe how well they fit together. But she wanted more. She wanted to be a part of him so much that she felt as if she might fly apart at any moment.

Like a faint sound during a thunderstorm, the inner voice telling her she was a fool didn't stand a chance. She had wanted revenge, and if she made Sam love her then hurt him as he had hurt her sister, wouldn't she have the sweetest revenge of all?

At the same time, Haley knew her desire had little to do with revenge. She wanted Sam to love her, pure and simple. For so long she'd had to ignore her own needs because someone else's were more urgent. She'd told herself she was happy to wait for the one special man, and she would know him when the time came. Was this the man and the time? Joel slept peacefully in his carrier just an arm's length away, the world could wait. Why not take something for herself, just this once?

As he continued to caress her, she could hardly hear for the thunder of blood in her ears. It drowned out further thought, gradually even her fear that she might be the one paying the price instead of Sam.

"Are you sure about this?" he asked.

There was only one possible answer. "Yes. Oh, yes."

She wanted him desperately, but couldn't keep her face from betraying anticipation of the pain to come. She told herself it would pass swiftly and then it would be glorious.

He reached into the pocket of his discarded jeans and fumbled with a small packet. Seeing what it was, she felt the enormity of what she was about to do hammer through her. She fought for calm. It would be all right. She loved Sam, she told herself. But as he began to ease himself over her, she caught her breath, unsuccessfully willing her tense muscles to relax.

Suddenly his heated gaze chilled with shock as he read the truth in her set face and wire-taut body. Abruptly he levered himself away from her. "This is the first time for you, isn't it?"

"Yes, but it's all right, honestly." She had never been more sure of anything.

"Honestly is an odd word to use, considering you've been anything but honest with me."

She wanted to scream in frustration. What did it matter if he was her first? Wasn't it enough that she had chosen him freely, with her whole heart? He had no need to hold back on her account. It would be all right, if only he was patient with her inexperience.

She started to tell him so, but the words died on her lips as her mind cleared. What had she done? He wasn't questioning her virginal state, as much as what it told him. She saw the knowledge invade his gaze, darkening his eyes to a smoldering hue.

She struggled upright, aflame with desires that would never be quenched, at least not by Sam. "You have to let me explain."

"Go right ahead," he said, his tone as chilly as a lake in winter. "I'd like to know how can you be a virgin and have a baby."

The embers of her passion died, leaving her drained. Why hadn't she stopped him before he found out the truth? The answer was as blinding as the joy he had made her feel. Until he knew everything, she had no chance of a future with him. Against all reason, she yearned for one.

Her body protested, but she made herself reach for

her clothes. She felt numb as she began to put them on. "Joel isn't my baby."

His cold tone sliced to her heart. "Obviously not. So who does he belong to?"

She took a deep breath to subdue the anguish threatening to consume her. "You," she said softly. "When I told you I had a sister named Ellen who died, I didn't tell you everything. She was the illustrator, Ellen Portman, and Joel was her baby. I adopted him after she passed away. You're Joel's father, Sam."

When his burning glare raked her, she forced herself not to look away. He couldn't be angrier with her than she was with herself for letting desire come before her duty. Nor was he going to intimidate her into backing down.

"So I'm Joel's father, am I?" he said, an edge of steel in his voice. "Well then that would require a miracle."

She stared at him. "What are you talking about?"

He stood up and his magnificence brought a lump to her throat. His anger froze her into immobility as he dressed with jerky movements. Then he grabbed her hand and hauled her to her feet. "Come with me. I'll show you what I'm talking about."

Chapter Seven

How could she have been so stupid? Haley asked herself as she followed him back to the house. The answer was blindingly clear. She had wanted him to make love to her so much that she had abandoned her carefully laid plan the moment he took her in his arms.

She understood how shocked he must be to discover that she had lied to him all along, after coming into his home under false pretenses. She remembered him explaining how his mother had lied to him about his father's death, and as a result, that he disliked being lied to. He had every right to hate her, she thought miserably. But it didn't explain his talk of miracles.

His attitude changed when she told him he was Joel's father, she recalled. So he still intended to deny it. Was it going to take a court order and a blood test to make him accept his responsibility? Surely he was a bigger man than that?

He stalked ahead of her, carrying Joel's baby carrier, the sleeping baby blissfully unaware of the drama unfolding around him. When Sam had picked the carrier up, she'd seen tenderness in his expression. Then had come anger and...something else. He looked like a man denied some special gift, she thought.

He obviously cared about the baby. He spent far more time with him than was strictly necessary, and enjoyed it. So why did he refuse to believe that he could be Joel's father?

It wasn't as if money or resources were a problem. His books were hugely successful, and Sam was a generous man. Earlier, when she had queried the name of a file on his computer, he had gruffly admitted that it related to a scholarship fund for his sister's children. She had found other files like it, suggesting that he made a point of sharing his wealth. She was at a loss to explain his reaction.

She remembered her friend, Miranda, asking if she was sure Sam was Joel's father. Doubt crept in, unnerving Haley until she shook it off. Ellen had never lied to her, and had no reason to do so when she knew she was dying. Anyway, the truth was visible to the naked eye. Joel was so like Sam that they couldn't be anything but father and son.

Growing angry, Haley quickened her pace until she caught up with Sam, and reached for the carrier. "I'll take him, since you no longer want anything to do with him.''

Sam's growl of negation startled her. "He's fine where he is."

"No, he's not," she said furiously, keeping her tone low so as not to disturb the sleeping baby. "His father just rejected him out of hand. How can any child be fine with that?" Sam had also rejected her, but later would do to deal with her own feelings. Now, all her concern was for Joel.

Sam's gaze was wintry, chilling her in spite of the sunshine. "You seem very sure of your facts."

"My sister wouldn't lie about something like that when she knew she was dying."

"I'm sorry," he said automatically. "It's a helluva tragedy, and I can understand grief making you desperate to find a home for Joel so you can get on with your life."

She had to clench her fists to keep from rearranging his handsome features. "I'm not desperate, nor is anyone taking Joel from me without a fight. But he deserves to know his father. She told me it was you, and I believe her."

His eyes filmed, then he shook his head. "If your sister was seriously ill, she might have been confused."

"Not about this. Do you deny sleeping with Ellen Portman a year and a half ago?"

"I don't deny it, because it's true. We'd been working together on and off for some time. The day my divorce became final, she was also upset about something. She wouldn't tell me what was the matter, but we ended up comforting each other. That's all there was to it.''

Haley glanced at the baby in the carrier and pain clamped around her heart. ''Obviously, there was a lot more to it.''

''Obviously, but it doesn't make me Joel's father.''

Rage fueled the urge to protect her sister's memory. ''Ellen didn't sleep around.''

His scowl deepened. ''I'm not saying she did. The Ellen I knew was sweet and gentle, more worried about what I was going through than her own problems. I knew she'd been sick, but never imagined it was terminal.''

''She didn't want pity.''

''And I didn't pity her. She was wonderful and talented.'' His voice broke as if he was having trouble dealing with Haley's thunderbolt. ''All I knew was that she needed me as much as I needed her. It never happened again.''

They had reached the house and Sam held the door open to allow Haley to go inside. As she brushed past him, she felt the electricity crackling between them, a disturbing reminder of all they could have shared. Her heart fell. No matter how much she yearned for the warmth of his embrace, nothing was likely to come of it now.

Telling herself it was a good thing didn't help. In spite of everything, desire clawed at her so fiercely that she wondered how she could have denied herself a man's love for so long.

How Ellen would smile if she knew, Haley thought, hearing her sister's "I told you so" as a dreamlike echo in her mind. Of all men, why did Sam have to be the one to shatter Haley's preconceptions? It was like having a door opened on a glimpse of paradise, only to have it close again moments later.

"I'll take Joel now. He'll be more comfortable in his crib," she said, needing time to recover her shattered composure.

"I'll come with you."

Did he think she would run away if he turned his back? She would have thought he'd be pleased to see her go. "There's no need," she said stiffly. "I'm not going anywhere just yet."

He inclined his head in agreement. "We have some things to straighten out first."

Then she could leave anytime, she heard although he didn't say it. The thought drove her to despair.

This wasn't what she'd planned at all. She had known he wouldn't acknowledge Joel willingly, and had come prepared to argue her case. What she hadn't allowed for was Sam's effect on her. It complicated everything.

You had plenty of warning, she told herself as she went through the motions of putting the sleeping baby to bed, struggling to ignore Sam leaning against the door frame, watching her every move. She had been immediately attracted to him. Thinking of the strength of her response, she swallowed hard. She had never felt anything so all-consuming in her life. If she'd had any sense, she would have run as fast as she could in the opposite direction.

Instead, she had insisted on confronting The Beast in his lair. Someone more experienced might have recognized the danger, but Haley wasn't experienced, as Sam had correctly guessed. She had been playing with fire, and hadn't had the sense to jump back before she got burned.

Well, she could learn from her mistakes, she resolved. From now on she would think of him as Joel's father and nothing more.

"Finished?" he asked, as she pulled a bunny rug over the baby.

"I'll sit here awhile, in case he wakes up."

Sam was beside her in an instant, taking her hand. "If he does, the baby monitor will alert you. We have some unfinished business."

She wanted to insist on remaining with Joel— where she was safe? She knew she didn't mean physically safe. She didn't fear Sam. But there were other kinds of danger, particularly to her emotions. The havoc he could cause them terrified her.

But he was already towing her out of the room. He closed the door quietly behind them, then steered her down the hall.

She had expected him to take her to his office, but they went to his study instead. It was the kind of place where he might simply come to think. The glorious view of the lake from the window made it ideal for quiet contemplation.

Contemplation was far from her mind now, as he

gestured for her to sit in a leather-bound chair along-side a rolltop desk. She felt like a schoolgirl summoned to the headmaster's office for a dressing-down. Except that Sam's closeness in the small room was anything but schoolmasterly. If he took her in his arms now, her resistance would be nonexistent, she knew.

Think of him as Joel's father, she reminded herself. As long as Sam refused to acknowledge his child, there could be nothing else between them.

She straightened her spine. "If you think I'm going to sit here while you lecture me, you're wrong. I should have told you who I was, and I apologize for that. But not for bringing Joel to you. He's entitled to know his father."

Sam loomed over her, clamping a hand on each arm of the chair, effectively imprisoning her. His face was like a thundercloud. "It's as well for you that I've never hit a woman in my life. Because right now, I'm more tempted than I've ever been."

She lifted her chin, refusing to be cowed. "Only a coward takes refuge in threats of violence."

"I don't make threats."

She knew she should shut up, before she provoked him beyond endurance. She wasn't afraid he would actually hit her. But he obviously wanted to do *something* and her heart sang as she realized what it was. "How do you deal with provocation, Sam?" she whispered, unable to hold the words back.

"Mostly, I yield to it." As she had hoped he would, he leaned forward and kissed her.

Trapped by his arms in the chair, she could only absorb the breathtaking impact of his mouth on hers. A chorus of need played through her as he grasped the back of her neck to deepen the kiss, making the room spin crazily around her.

He's Joel's father, nothing more, she told herself desperately, but the thought slid away on the mindless cusp of a thousand sensations. Reason was swept away. Sanity wavered. She would have been content to have him go on kissing her forever.

Liar, she chided herself. She wanted much more from him than a kiss.

When he pulled away, his eyes were smoky with desire, but it quickly gave way to anger. At her or at himself? Both, she decided, consoled that she wasn't the only one letting temptation drown out common sense.

"Why did you do that?" she asked when the room stopped spinning.

"It was the safer option." Without elaborating, Sam dropped into the chair behind the desk and dragged air into his lungs, wondering why he suddenly had trouble breathing. He hadn't meant to kiss Haley again. But he had needed to. It was becoming a bad habit.

He had a quick flashback to the gazebo, when she had accepted his caresses so willingly. He had seen the trepidation in her eyes, and the trust. It had confused him until the reason came to him with blinding clarity. Unbidden, desire stirred again, clamoring for satiation. Clamoring for her. She hadn't lied about wanting him, he'd swear. But she had lied about everything else.

He welcomed the anger, letting it dampen his desire. A lie was the one thing he wouldn't tolerate. "Who are you, really? The truth this time."

He made himself focus on her answer, although it was hard with her lips still rosy from his kiss. Her eyes blazed a challenge back at him. "As I told you, my name is Haley Glen and I work as a freelance business consultant."

"You're not employed by Miranda's agency."

She shook her head. "Miranda didn't want me to take this job. And I tried to talk you into hiring someone else, remember?"

"Don't try to pin this on me," he growled. "You lied your way in so you could spin your cock-and-bull tale about me fathering your sister's child."

Her hands trembled before she linked them in her lap. "It isn't cock-and-bull, it's the truth."

"No way. It's a physical impossibility."

He hunted through the desk until he found an envelope bearing the address of his former brother-in-law's medical practice, and spun the package across the desk to her. "Read that."

"I don't…"

"Read it."

His command, delivered with the force of a rifleshot, made her jump. She opened the envelope and retrieved the report it contained. He hadn't looked at it for months, but he knew the contents by heart. Several times he'd been tempted to burn the report, but had kept it as a reminder to avoid serious entanglements in future.

"Does it or does it not show a sperm count low enough to rule out any chance that I'm Joel's father?" he demanded.

She looked up, bewilderment clouding her lovely eyes. "I don't understand."

He refused to let her tragic expression sway him. "What's not to understand? I can't give any woman a child, not my ex-wife, and certainly not your sister."

"But Ellen was so sure."

She was getting to him in spite of his determination not to allow it. "You said she was ill. What happened?"

"The tumor was diagnosed soon after the two of you met at that business function. She became too sick to work on the first Panda book, but went into remission and was well enough to illustrate the second book. Because of the treatment she'd had, she didn't think she could get pregnant. She wanted the baby more than her own life. In the end, that's what it cost her."

Seeing Haley's unhappiness felt like a knife in his own heart, but he fought the temptation to take her in his arms. She and her sister had tried to take him for a ride. He should throw her out on her ear, not feel such a strong urge to comfort her that his arms ached with the effort not to touch her.

Unable to stand the sight of her misery a moment longer he said, "Toward the end, your sister may well have convinced herself she was telling the truth. Why she singled me out, I don't know, but she was wrong.''

Haley let the report flutter to the desktop. She felt cold, numb. The thought that Joel would never know his father weighed heavily on her. It was bad enough that she had been estranged from her father, but at least she'd spoken to him, visited him. Joel would never have even that much.

She struggled to keep her voice level. ''Could there be a mistake?''

He shook his head. ''The doctor who ran the test is my ex-wife's brother. We may have hated each other's guts but he's at the top of his field.''

Haley knew she was clutching at straws, but this wasn't making sense. Her sister hadn't been involved with any other man for two years. She had been too ill. Then when she had gone into remission, she hadn't been confident enough of her future to date anyone.

Ellen said that she had only slept with Sam that one time. By then, she was pregnant and had moved in with Haley. How could she have been involved with anyone else without Haley knowing?

''If this man didn't like you, could he have rigged the test results?'' she asked hesitantly.

''He's a doctor. They take an oath.'' Sam replaced the report in the envelope. ''This isn't getting us anywhere. I'd like to help, but...''

But he didn't intend to, she saw, feeling her heart sink. She didn't blame him. He wasn't responsible for another man's child. Nor for Haley's reaction to him. "I understand. I'll leave first thing in the morning."

Sam knew he should let her leave, but instead he said, "I don't want you to go."

Her startled gaze flew to his face. "But surely, after all this…"

"I can't damn you for doing what you think is right," he conceded. "I overreacted to finding out you'd lied to me."

"I understand why you hate being deceived," she said, wishing with all her heart that she'd chosen a different course of action. Haley also understood why he had been so furious with Ellen when she told him about the baby. Knowing that he couldn't possibly be the baby's father, he had assumed Ellen was also lying to him. Haley sighed. "I didn't mean to reopen old wounds."

"You weren't to know."

Even if he wasn't Joel's father, there was still the question of whether or not he had stolen the idea for his best-selling character from her sister. Proving it would be easier under his roof. So would spending more time in his arms. "I'll stay," she said, knowing which reason mattered most to her.

"Good, because I have another proposition for you."

She could almost see his thoughts spinning. "What is it?"

"I want you to marry me."

Haley felt her jaw drop. At the same time, she felt a powerful wave of reaction grip her. What would it be like being married to Sam, sharing his bed, his life? He might not be Joel's biological parent, but she had seen enough to know he would be a wonderful father. That he would also be a wonderful lover, she also didn't doubt.

She drove the seductive images away, although her physical response was harder to ignore. ''Marry you? Are you out of your mind?'' Was she out of hers for even considering it. Yet she knew that was precisely what she was doing.

''It's a logical suggestion,'' he said, sounding more like he was developing a plot than proposing marriage. ''Knowing I can't father children, I had made up my mind not to risk marrying again. But you already have a son you regard as your own child, so I won't be cheating you of anything. Nor myself.'' His tone softened. ''I know exactly how you feel about Joel. I'm starting to feel the same way about him. He'll be the son I never dreamed I could have. And you'd have someone who will accept him as part of your life. I gather you've had something of a struggle since you've had him.''

Miranda, she thought furiously. Sam must have asked her friend about her. Haley had spoken to Miranda herself several times since coming to work for Sam, but she had carefully avoided any mention of the sparks flying between them. Miranda must have drawn her own conclusions. She also wasn't above doing a bit of matchmaking, Haley noted. ''I manage,'' she said shortly. She would not be seen as some kind of charity case.

"I know, and you're doing remarkably well. But wouldn't it be better *not* to have such a struggle, for Joel's sake, if not for your own?"

He had said the one thing guaranteed to make her consider his proposal, the one thing that had brought them together in the first place. She wanted to give her baby so much more than she was able to provide. Not only material things, but a family life as well. Sam could give them both that.

As the thought arose, she realized how much she wanted it for herself, too. With an estranged father, and a mother and stepfather who meant well but were less mature than Haley herself, she had never known the kind of love, warmth and security that other families took for granted.

Her family had leaned on *her,* instead of the other way around. During Ellen's illness and afterward, most of the burden had fallen on Haley. It had never occurred to her mother or stepfather that they might take a hand in their grandchild's upbringing. They had left it all to Haley.

She loved Joel too much to mind, but occasionally it would be nice to have someone she could lean on, she thought. She had almost decided it was an impossible dream. After her experience with Richard Cross, she had all but ruled out marriage for herself. Unlike Richard, Sam had never made her feel as if the baby was an intrusion. He never would, she sensed.

His solution was so tempting that an acceptance hovered on her lips. Until she thought of what he *wasn't* offering. Love. If she married him, he would be a passionate lover. This afternoon's experience told her how sublime it could be between them. The very thought triggered a volcanic reaction deep within her. But making love to her wasn't the same as loving her. Could she commit to a lifetime of purely physical rapport?

Before she could answer, Joel's plaintive cries sounded through the receiver of the baby monitor that Sam had plugged in before he dropped his bombshell. "Go to him," he urged. "Take care of the baby's needs first, then think it over and give me your answer."

It was this consideration that decided her. "I've already thought it over, and I will marry you, Sam, as soon as you want me to."

Chapter Eight

Predictably, Miranda was delighted and bubbling with ideas. "One of my clients is a cousin of the fashion designer, Aloys Gada. If he puts in a good word for you, Gada will design a wedding dress to make you drool," she said over the phone.

Haley began to pace, glad that the phone was cordless. "We're only having a quiet ceremony with you and Sam's agent as witnesses, with a party later for family and friends. So I won't need a designer wedding dress." It didn't stop her picturing it, but it didn't fit the businesslike nature of the agreement she had made with Sam.

Miranda picked up the wistfulness in Haley's voice. "It doesn't sound very romantic."

"It isn't like that between Sam and me."

"You do love him, don't you?" Haley knew her

silence spoke volumes. "Oh, Haley, you *do* love him.
I can hear the catch in your breathing."

Haley tried to make light of it. "Maybe I tripped
over a rug."

"And maybe you fell headlong for Sam. Doesn't
he feel the same way?"

"We're marrying because it suits us both. He'll be
a wonderful husband and father." She didn't want to
betray Sam's confidence by sharing his reasons, even
with her closest friend, but she had already explained
to Miranda that Sam wasn't Joel's biological father,
after all.

"I guess you know what's right for you," Miranda
admitted. "I'm glad I'm to be a witness, at least."

"It will be fine," Haley assured her. Would it, she
wondered after she hung up? She hadn't told Miranda, but since agreeing to marry Sam a week ago,
Haley had faced the truth herself. He might not love
her, but she loved him.

She had always thought when she fell in love, it
would come as a bolt out of the blue. With Sam, it
was more gradual, emphasized by the many small
considerations he showed her. He hadn't tried to
make love to her again, assuring her that he was content to wait until their wedding night. That alone had
brought a lump to her throat. How had he known so
exactly, what she wanted?

He had somehow understood that the moment in
the gazebo when she had almost let him make love
to her had been out of character. She had always
meant to save herself for marriage. Had she sensed

that Sam would be the one? It was the only reason she could think of for letting him go further than any other man she'd known. Not that she'd been thinking very rationally.

"Mindless passion" was the right term, she thought. He'd driven her out of her mind with need for him, until nothing else had mattered. When he touched her, it still didn't. His kisses drove her to heights she had never known she could reach. Now he was away at a meeting and Haley missed him so much that it was almost painful.

Hard to believe she had known him less than a month altogether. She felt as if he had always been part of her life. He might not love her now, but he would in time, she was convinced. How could he not share the sense of rightness she felt with him?

What had become of The Beast? Ellen's nickname for him seemed inappropriate now. Knowing that he couldn't be Joel's father, Haley had tried to let go of her questions, although she would always wonder about her sister's unknown lover. But Sam would be all the father the baby needed. And all the husband Haley herself desired.

And increasingly her suspicion that Sam had stolen her sister's idea seemed unlikely now that Haley knew him better. She had made up her mind not to take her investigation any further. Ellen would have approved. She had hated suspicion and intrigue of any kind, and would far rather have helped Haley to plan her wedding than hunt for proof of Sam's wrongdoing.

How she missed Ellen now. Haley blinked hard. Her sister lived on in Joel, she reminded herself. She picked the precious baby up and held him close. "You have your mother's big, blue eyes, did you know?"

He widened them at her and she lost herself in their depths. How could anyone look so wise yet so innocent, all at once. "Da, da, ba ba," he chattered.

She tickled him. "Da da, ba ba to you, too."

He giggled, showing a tiny mound of white in his pink gum. "Look, your very first tooth is almost through. Aren't you a clever boy."

The warmth in her voice made Joel bounce happily in her arms. "Wait until we show your new daddy."

Happiness spun through her. From now on, there would always be someone to share the milestones in Joel's life, and in her own. "You can't wait, and neither can I," she assured the baby. "But right now, it's time I tucked you into bed. You need all your strength to grow more of those pearly little teeth."

He yawned on cue and she laughed as she carried him to his room, Dougal trotting at her heels. Once there, the dog sprawled across the doorway, having appointed himself Joel's guardian. If the baby stirred, Dougal would come to find Haley to alert her. He only pried himself from the baby's side when Sam was at home, then she could almost see the dog's frustration as he tried to divide his loyalties.

The baby didn't protest when she settled him in his crib, proving her point. He was tired. She debated taking a nap herself, but knew she wouldn't sleep until Sam came home. She would get some work done instead.

Before she left the room, she switched on the baby monitor so she would be able to hear Joel from Sam's office. Then she recalled that Sam had plugged the other speaker into the study when he minded Joel for her while she washed her hair last night. It was still there. Should she rely on Dougal, or fetch the receiver?

She tousled the dog's ears. "It's not that I don't trust you, but I'll get the speaker. If you ever father pups, you'll understand."

She hadn't been in the study since the night Sam proposed marriage to her. As she opened the door, the memory surged back. Was it only a week ago? She caressed the green leather of his antique chair. It looked as if it had belonged to generations of Wintons. The thought gave her a reassuring sense of continuity.

The monitor receiver was on the desk, almost buried under Sam's paperwork. She sighed. As fast as she got his office organized, he created a new jumble somewhere else. She didn't feel confident enough yet to tidy his private sanctuary without invitation, so steeled herself to ignore the mess.

The speaker cord was tangled under the desk. She dropped to her knees to untangle it from a stack of folders. They toppled at her touch and she recognized the handwriting on one of them. It was Ellen's.

Her hand shook as she reached for it. This must be some of the work Ellen and Sam had done together.

She had to look, to feel closer to her sister for just a minute. Settling on the floor with her back against the desk, she opened the folder.

Ellen's style had always been distinctive. With only a few deft lines, she had been able to breathe life into an animal or a magical creature. These were sketches of Australian native animals, but so human-looking that Haley smiled. Who wouldn't love a kangaroo with a patch pocket instead of a pouch, and adorable twin joeys? Written on the sketches was 'Cosmic Panda and the Bush Babies'.

Haley leafed through the sketches until she came to a single sheet of coffee-stained paper. As she turned it over, her breath snagged. Drawn on the back of a menu for a function dated three years beforehand, the sketches incorporated features that she recognized as part of Cosmic Panda's present-day look.

Haley knew she must be looking at the birth of Sam's famous character, created by her sister's unmistakable hand on the first night she and Sam crossed paths. Ellen's notes littered the sketches. An idea for a prop here, an expression there, even story notes, suitably illustrated, everything Sam needed to write the story and claim the credit.

It was true.

Dread filled Haley. Since Sam's proposal of marriage, she had decided that Ellen had been joking when she said she should share the royalties from the books. As their creator, she should have shared a lot more. Her child should have shared more. Haley decided.

Thinking of Joel, Haley felt her heart trip. If Sam could hide this, had he told the truth about not being able to father children? She had seen the medical report, but she knew as well as anyone what could be created on a computer.

Then she remembered the soul-deep sadness in his eyes. No one could fake such emotion. Even if he'd been truthful about Joel, he had lied about creating the panda character. Haley had the proof right here in her hands.

And wished with all her heart that she didn't.

She didn't want to accept that the man she loved had let her sister struggle while he prospered from her ideas. Haley was tempted to shove the folder back into the stack and pretend she hadn't seen it. But it would be there like a time bomb, ready to explode the moment their marriage hit a rough patch.

"What are you doing?"

She looked up, startled to find Sam looming over her, his face like thunder. Dougal stood behind him, his tail thumping furiously. "I didn't hear you come in."

"Obviously not. I looked in on Joel. He's still asleep."

He wasn't going to make her into the guilty party, she resolved. He was the one with some explaining to do. "I know. I was listening on the monitor," she said as she scrambled to her feet, the folder clutched in her hand.

"While you did what? Snooped through my study?"

His tone cut through her bravado. He sounded so angry that she flinched. "I wasn't snooping. You left the monitor receiver in here and I came to get it."

"It was on the desk, not under it."

"The cord was tangled." How pathetic it sounded now, although it was the truth. She straightened. "I found this."

She held out the folder but he hardly glanced at it. "I know what it is."

"If you know, then…"

His brows forked downward in a scowl. "The point is, do *you* know what it is?"

How she wished she didn't. "It's my sister's original designs for the character you claim to have invented."

His scowl deepened, and she glimpsed something else in his dark gaze. Disappointment? How could he be disappointed in Haley, when *he* had let *her* down?

"I gather you think I didn't," he said heavily.

She would rather have cut out her own tongue than admit, "What else can I think?"

He turned away, his broad shoulders set in an unrelenting line. "Nothing that would change what you apparently think of me. I suppose you're happy now?"

Odd word to use when she felt so tormented that she wanted to scream. She ached to have him cradle her against his hard chest. Instead she kept her head high. "Why should I be happy?"

"Because you finally found something to pin on

me. Since Joel's paternity doesn't fit the bill, you kept searching until you found something else."

She turned away, staring blindly at a picture on the wall. "You make it sound as if all I want is revenge."

"Don't you?" His hands dropped to her shoulders and he spun her so she couldn't avoid facing him. His gaze heated her blood even as it accused. "I can't deny hurting your sister, but only because I thought she wanted to manipulate me into supporting a child I knew couldn't possibly be mine."

Compassion for him flooded Haley, but she shook it off. "That doesn't explain these drawings."

Frustration sparked in his gaze. "You really think I would steal her ideas?"

"I don't know what to think any more." Not about that, or her feelings toward him, or a thousand other things. He confused her, exhilarated her, set her pulse roaring and her heart pounding. He could kiss her senseless, make her want him as she had never wanted any other man, and plunge her to the depths of despair, all in the space of a few minutes. "If you'd just explain…"

"Explain what? Why I made a fortune out of someone else's ideas? Or why I claimed all the credit? That's what you're really saying isn't it?"

I don't want it to be true, she thought wildly, understanding that he wasn't going to explain. She hadn't realized how much she had wanted him to restore her shattered faith, so she could go on loving him without reservation.

She still did, she accepted with a sinking heart.

Nothing he did could make her stop loving him. It was as much a part of her now as breathing. Knowing he didn't feel the same only made it harder.

"I wish I'd never set eyes on this," she said bitterly.

His expression hardened. "That makes two of us."

Disappointment speared her. "Is that all you intend to say?"

His look of disdain made her shudder. "There is something else. I thought over your comment about my former brother-in-law disliking me enough to falsify my medical report. The next day, I consulted another doctor and had the test repeated."

Every other thought fled from her mind. "What did he say?"

"I've just come from his office with the results. You were right."

Relief for him flooded through her. "Then you can...you're not..."

"I'm not sterile and I can father children. I always could. On the way home I called my ex-brother-in-law to demand an explanation. He said that test results can be wrong for lots of reasons. When I asked him if my ex-wife hadn't wanted to spoil her model figure by having children, his silence gave me my answer. She knew I wanted a family, but rather than be honest, she had her brother put the blame on me. It was easier than admitting that she never wanted children all along."

"How could she do such a thing?"

"Piling on the agony seems to be a peculiarly female art."

She recoiled from the coldness in his voice, knowing it wasn't directed at only his former wife and her brother. She could imagine Sam's high spirits as he hurried home, eager to share his news with her, only to meet with accusations.

Sam was made to have children of his own. Did his ex-wife have any idea of the extent of her cruelty? Of all the ways she could have protected her vanity, convincing him he was sterile had to be the lowest. Haley was glad he had finally discovered the truth.

As well as Joel, she had seen him with his young fans in the press and on television. One news story had shown him thrusting through a throng of parents to crouch beside a nine-year-old boy who desperately wanted to show Sam a book he had written. The effort might have been amateurish, but Sam handled the work like gold, praising and encouraging until the boy glowed with pleasure.

"Regardless of what you think, I'm happy for you," she said.

His eyes sparked with anger. "You have a strange way of showing it."

Haley wished he would say something, offer some explanation for the drawings instead of letting her think the worst.

But it wasn't the worst, not by a long stretch. "This means there is every chance that Joel is my child, after all. The brand of protection I used that day was subject to a recall because a batch was faulty. It didn't concern me as long as I believed I was sterile. But it has to be the reason Joel was conceived. As soon as our relationship is established beyond doubt, I intend to seek custody.''

She felt the color drain from her face. "You can't take him from me."

"He's my son," he said as if it was already fact. "You've just shown me how far I can trust you. Joel will be better off with someone who isn't working to a hidden agenda."

She squared her shoulders. "I'm not proud of deceiving you, but at least I did it for Joel, not for my own gain."

His slashing gesture included the damning folder on the desk. "And you think I claimed your sister's work as my own for money?"

"What other explanation is there?"

Something dark shimmered in his gaze. "None you're prepared to hear."

"Why won't you try me?" The words came out as a plea. Why wouldn't he help her to understand? She desperately wanted a lifeline, but his expression made it clear he wasn't going to throw her one. She was on her own, to believe him or not as she chose.

His mouth tilted into a humorless smile. "Odd words to use, considering you've already tried me and found me guilty.

How could she argue with the truth? "I'm sorry, Sam."

"I'm sorry, too. More than you know."

The finality she heard was almost her undoing. "What are you going to do?"

He set his jaw. "I understand your wish to remain part of Joel's life. You're the only mother he's known and he loves you," he continued, his tone not softening in the slightest degree.

At least he understood. But she also loved Sam, too, in spite of everything, tormented beyond belief to find herself so opposed to him. Dear heaven, how could she feel this way, when he was threatening everything she held dear? "You know I'll fight you. I won't have Joel handed back and forth like a parcel, between our households."

"That won't be necessary. My proposal still stands. Married, we can parent Joel together, no matter how we feel about each other."

Nothing had changed, she saw as she fought to clear her fogged mind. She had known that Sam didn't love her when he proposed. She had accepted, hoping that he would gradually come to share her feelings. Now there was no chance of it happening. She wavered. Could she commit to marrying him without the slenderest hope that he would come to love her?

If she didn't, she would lose Joel. Her vow to fight Sam in court was no bluff, but her resources would only stretch so far. In a war of attrition, Sam would win.

She knew defeat showed on her face. "You don't give me much choice."

His lip curled into a sneer. "It's a lot more leeway than you're giving me."

She glanced at the folder. "For what it's worth, I don't believe you stole Cosmic Panda. I don't know what these drawings mean, but there must be some other explanation."

"Big of you," he murmured.

"Sam, don't, please?"

His eyebrow canted upward. "Don't what? Defend myself? Or expect you to give me the benefit of the doubt? I'll survive without your good opinion, but I won't have you poisoning my son's mind with your nasty suspicions."

She fiddled with a pen on the desk. "I would never do that."

He looked at her for a long time. "No, I believe you wouldn't. You're a mystery to me, Haley. How can someone so beguiling have so many hidden agendas?"

"I have only one. To protect my baby." Everything she had done was for her child. Except perhaps one. Accepting Sam's proposal had more to do with her own needs than with Joel's.

Sam nodded tautly. "Then we're in accord on that, at least. After I left the doctor's office, I was walking on air. Champagne didn't seem adequate, so I decided to buy you this." His tone suggested he regretted the impulse now.

From his pocket, he withdrew a small square box. He flipped it open and she gasped. Inside was the most exquisite engagement ring she had ever seen.

Through misty eyes she took in the magnificent marquise-cut diamond set in two strands of entwined gold and platinum. It shone with the light of a thousand suns.

A lump rose in her throat, but it was nothing compared to the sensation she felt when Sam lifted her left hand and slid the ring onto her finger.

If only he had chosen it as a symbol of his love, instead of sealing what amounted to a business arrangement. "It looks real," she whispered.

"I can show you the valuation certificate if you like."

His coldness was like a slap in the face. She choked back a denial. Better he should think she meant the value of the stone rather than the value of the moment, she thought. "There's no need. It's lovely. How did you know my ring size?"

"I wound a strand of your hair around your finger and estimated from that."

There was only one time when he could have done it, and that was when he almost made love to her down by the lake. The thought shook her. How close had he come to having real feelings for her, until finding her apparently snooping in his study?

The folder. He had neatly avoided explaining that, she thought with a pang. If there was a logical explanation, why wouldn't he share it with her? She didn't believe he was capable of stealing someone else's ideas, but until he told her what really happened, she was stuck with her suspicion.

He wanted her trust, but he wasn't prepared to trust

her, she thought furiously. So be it. She gathered up the receiver for the baby monitor. "I'd better get back to work."

His hand on her arm stayed her. "You've done enough."

Sensation bolted through her like summer lightning. "You're firing me?"

He shook his head. "Now that we're officially engaged, you're to think of this as your home, not your workplace. You may as well start now."

"But the job isn't finished yet."

"It is for you. From now on, your job is to be my wife and the mother of my son." For the first time since he walked in, his expression mellowed. She had no illusion that it was on her account. His next words proved it. "It feels strange, saying that. My son. I have a son."

"You haven't had him tested yet," she reminded him gently.

"I don't have to. I've felt the bond since the moment you brought him to me. I've always liked being around children, but with Joel it's different. He feels like...like part of me. Now I understand why."

She fiddled with the monitor cord. "He seems to recognize you, too."

Sam preened slightly. "He does, doesn't he?" Then his face underwent a rapid change. "My lord, to think I was nearly denied that relationship because of one woman's vanity."

Haley felt little sympathy for his ex-wife. "Are you going to take it further?"

"Sue her and her brother, you mean? I wouldn't waste my energy. Do you believe in the old saying, 'what goes around, comes around'?"

She nodded. "It's usually true in my experience."

"Then the two of them will get their comeuppance one way or another. If there's any justice, one day her biological clock will go crazy, but it will be too late."

The writer in him couldn't help thinking in plots, Haley thought. "Stranger things have happened," she agreed.

He made a slashing gesture. "I don't really care. I have my son now, and I'm perfectly healthy."

And his male pride in his own potency was restored. She pictured Sam initiating his son into the male mysteries, his own place as alpha male secure again. He would be good at it, she thought. Joel was lucky to have such a devoted father.

Nevertheless, a fierce possessiveness welled up, causing her to clutch a hand to her breast. In agreeing to marry Sam, she had agreed to share Joel with him without thinking the consequences all the way through. As soon as Sam had medical proof of his paternity, Haley would be relegated to a non-blood relation, an outsider in her child's life. She could have borne that more easily if Sam would only say he loved her. Knowing he didn't made the situation almost intolerable.

"I know I'm asking you to give up a lot," he said as if reading her mind. "I'll make sure you don't regret it. Miranda told me how hard you've worked to provide for Joel. I'll make sure you never have to struggle for anything again.''

"I've done it willingly," she assured him, hating him to think her sacrifice had been less than whole-hearted.

"I'm aware of that, too, and as his father, I'm more grateful than I can say. If there's anything I can do to repay you, I will."

Love me, she thought, knowing it was the one thing he wouldn't do. "I don't require payment," she said stiffly. "All I want is the chance to be with my baby and watch him grow up."

Moisture sheened his gaze. "On this at least, we're in complete agreement."

Chapter Nine

How had he gotten himself into this? Sam wondered
as he watched preparations being made for the television interview he had agreed to record at his sister's
house. As usual, he had been too softhearted for his
own good. The reporter, Tanya Bolton, had gone to
school with his sister, Jessie, and she had asked him
to do it as a favor. Nothing else would have persuaded
him to give up his Saturday to this thankless task.

Jessie hadn't told Tanya about his engagement. The
leak had come from the jeweler where Sam had
bought the ring. Evidently the sales assistant had recognized Sam when he'd entered the shop. In high
spirits after getting the all-clear from the doctor, he
hadn't been as discreet as usual, and when the assistant had asked his fiancée's name, he had stupidly
given it. The assistant had called the TV station, and

Tanya had ferreted out the rest of the story, then prevailed on Jessie to ask him to grant her an exclusive.

He didn't plan on telling Tanya the real reason for the engagement. Like Jessie, the reporter believed they were in love and for Joel's sake, he wouldn't disillusion them.

After he explained to his sister about Joel's background, she had taken the baby to her heart. Joel was only a little younger than Jessie's own youngest, Jason, and the two babies found each other fascinating.

He glanced at the pair, cooing and chattering in baby language in a playpen in the shade of a silky oak tree. Jessie's husband had taken two-year-old Lauren to see a butterfly exhibition or she'd have been fussing over the babies like a little mother, Sam knew. Something stirred deep inside him as he imagined having a daughter as beautiful as Lauren. Or Haley.

It was her turn in the spotlight, the reporter having decided to interview them separately. Sam hadn't liked the idea. Since he threatened to seek full custody of his son, Haley had been cold and withdrawn around him. Putting a microphone in front of her and asking her to talk about Sam was akin to giving her a loaded gun. Would she take the opportunity to fire it at him? If she did, the headlines would be really something.

She was more likely to hold back to protect the baby than out of consideration for him. It didn't please him to think so. He'd rather she stood by him because she wanted to.

He was surprised how much he had missed their closeness. When she had agreed to marry him, she hadn't cared that he couldn't give her children. She had responded so passionately that heat banked inside him at the memory. She had seemed so different from his ex-wife. Finding Haley spying on him, ready to think the worst, had shaken his faith in her.

Why hadn't he told her about the drawings? They concerned her sister, so Haley was entitled to know. He knew it was because he had wanted her trust without having to explain himself. Finding it withheld, he had seen red.

He told himself he didn't care what she thought of him. She was a means to an end—custody of his son. He hadn't told Haley in case she misunderstood and thought he was trying to take Joel from her, but he had already set the wheels in motion. He wanted legal claim to Joel as soon as he could. It wouldn't change the baby's relationship with Haley, this was just something Sam needed to do for himself.

Last week, the test results had proved it. Joel was his child. His son. Would he ever get used to that? After more than a year of thinking he would never be able to say it, he had to deal with the living, breathing reality of a life he had helped to create. A life that was his responsibility from now on. He wouldn't take it lightly. Sam's father had been the most important person in his life. He wanted Joel to think the same about him one day.

He had meant it when he said he didn't want to shut Haley out of Joel's life. She had sacrificed too much, endured too much, and loved the baby too much for Sam to want to come between them.

But he recognized that he wanted more.

He wanted her love for himself. He wanted her to look at him with the same greedy gaze with which she looked at Joel. For the baby, it was a maternal hunger to hold on to the closeness they now shared. With Sam, it would be a grown-up hunger, the kind he knew how to satisfy beyond her wildest dreams.

Thinking of how it would be when they finally made love, beads of sweat broke out on his forehead. Jessie appeared with a glass of ice water. "You look like you need this."

He took it from her with a smile, glad she couldn't read his mind. "Thanks. You could fry eggs under these lights."

She nodded. "I've never understood why they need lights outdoors. But I guess Tanya knows her business. I'm sorry I got you into this, but she was very persuasive."

"I'd rather give your friend an exclusive than have a media feeding frenzy," he said.

His sister looked at Haley, sitting patiently under the lights. "Does Haley know what she's getting herself into?"

"She knows." More than Jessie ever suspected. "She can handle it, she's tough."

His sister frowned. "Not as tough as you think. I heard her having a little weep to herself when she was changing Joel and thought no one was within earshot. Did you two have a fight?"

The thought of Haley in tears did strange things to Sam's insides. He shook his head. "Maybe she was nervous about the interview."

"And maybe she's worried about the two of you. Treat her gently, big brother. She's worth it."

His sister moved away to attend to the babies, leaving Sam deep in thought. So Haley shed tears in private. He wanted to think it was over Joel, but she knew he'd never come between them, so it had to be something else. Because of him? That would mean she cared about him. Her actions—and unwillingness to trust him—suggested that she didn't.

He'd also believed he couldn't have kids, and been proved wrong. What else could he be wrong about?

He'd been listening to the interview with half attention. Suddenly that changed with Tanya's next question. "What brought you and Sam together?"

Tension ricocheted through him. He wasn't ashamed of how Joel had been conceived, or of how he had behaved afterward. As far as he had known then, he was doing the right thing. But depending on how she put it, Haley could make him sound like the greatest heel in existence.

Objectively, he couldn't blame her if she did. She must know it was her only chance of beating him in a custody fight. But he hoped she wouldn't. Not only for Joel's sake, but because Sam knew it would hurt like hell to hear her tear him down.

When had it become so important what she thought of him? About the same time he'd started obsessing about details such as the way she smelled of gardenias. And the ready way her mouth yielded under his.

He couldn't get enough of her.

He had promised himself he wouldn't fall in love again. He didn't need another woman using him, manipulating him. Haley had tried to do both. Schemed to get under his roof, into his life. Still thought he was capable of stealing other people's ideas.

Not entirely true, he told himself in fairness. He was the one who had wanted her under his roof. In his bed would be better, but it was a start. And he had seen the desperate plea in her eyes for him to explain about the drawings. If he hadn't stubbornly refused, it wouldn't be an issue between them. Was he using it to keep some distance between them?

Before he could continue down that road, Haley answered the question. "I was attracted to Sam from the moment we met. I thought then, he was a man I could love."

"And has time proved you right?"

Sam's insides clenched as Haley paused. He had to know. Did she love him? She gave the interviewer as tormented a look as Sam had ever seen. "Yes," she whispered.

Something broke inside Sam. The confession had sounded as if it was torn from her, as if it was the last thing she wanted to feel. He scowled, knowing what that was like. He jumped to his feet, determined to get her alone and have this out with her.

But the interviewer forestalled him. "Wonderful interview, Haley. All the very best for the future.

Sam, we'll have to hurry and get your segment in the can before this storm breaks.''

He could only allow himself to be shepherded into the circle of light, while Haley walked away without looking back.

Haley picked up Joel and hurried inside Jessie's house. She told herself the baby needed changing, but it wasn't the reason she wanted to get away from Sam.

Her mood felt as tempestuous as the storm threatening to break overhead. How could she have forgotten where she was? She had allowed Tanya to lull her into forgetting that this wasn't a cozy chat between friends, and had confessed on camera that she loved Sam. To herself she couldn't deny it any longer. But did she have to confess it to the world?

Thinking of Sam's face when he heard it, she felt a chill seep through her. He hadn't looked as if he welcomed the news.

He had looked the way her father had looked when she told him she wanted to spend more time with him, she recalled. As if she had imposed on him by asking.

What was it about her that drove away the people she loved? she asked herself. Was she so hard to love that they couldn't wait to get her out of their lives?

She told herself she was being melodramatic. Sam did want her in his life, as his partner and the mother of his child. It wasn't his fault that she had complicated things by falling in love with him. Joel

squirmed and chattered as if reminding her that he
was the sole reason Sam wanted to marry her.

"None of this is your fault," she told the baby,
tickling the soft folds of his tummy. He chuckled approvingly and kicked his legs. "You're still the number one man in my life."

But was he? Or had a tall, broad-shouldered writer
usurped that role? Her vision veiled and she blinked
to clear it. "Next thing, I'll be looking for one of
your daddy's happy endings," she said to Joel.
"Where's Cosmic Panda when we need him?" But
he was only a fiction, like her engagement to Sam.

Since the night he proposed, she had tried to keep
her distance, telling herself she should start as she
meant to go on. He hadn't seemed to mind, continu-
ing his normal routine as if becoming engaged was
an everyday event. Haley was the one whose heart
felt as if it was about to shatter into little pieces every
time their paths crossed. Since they were sharing the
house, it was almost unavoidable. Mealtimes were the
worst, when she was forced to make small talk as if
everything was fine, when her heart felt as if it was
breaking.

Whenever he came into a room, she felt a dizzying
rush of love for him, wishing he would take her in
his arms and tell her he felt the same way. Remembering the way he kissed her, she felt hunger gnaw at
her. She wanted him so much that it hurt.

Instead, he greeted her coolly and asked about her
day. Sometimes he talked about his work, but mostly

they discussed unimportant things until she wanted to scream with frustration.

He was wonderful with Joel, though. She had never seen a more devoted father. Even the most unsavory tasks enthralled him, perhaps because he had never expected to be doing them.

She remembered the excitement on his face the first time he got Joel to burp after feeding him. You would think man had just landed on the moon.

Bathing Joel was another minor miracle to Sam. He hadn't minded getting soaked to the skin, his designer shirts plastered to his chest and baby powder clinging to his hair. Thinking of how attractive he looked bathing the baby, Haley felt her muscles clench in reaction.

She didn't want these feelings. Not when she knew they were one-sided. Too bad she had no idea how to stop them.

She finished changing the baby and picked him up. "Thank goodness I have you, pumpkin." She swung him high into the air and he gurgled in delight. "Joel's an airplane. Up, up into the sky he goes. Where he lands, nobody knows."

It was Joel's favorite game. His single-toothed grin widened as she swooped him through the air, imitating a plane. Her spirits edged upward. How could she complain about anything as long as she had Joel?

A polite knock caught her attention. Panting, she swung around, the baby in her arms. A stranger stood in the open doorway. He was tall and angular, the pants of his business suit a fraction too short for his spindly legs. Not one of the television crew, she decided, not sure how she knew. "Can I help you?"

The man gestured with his briefcase. "I'm looking for Sam. His agent told me I'd find him here. He impressed on me the urgency of getting these documents to him as soon as I could."

Her curiosity stirred. "He's recording a TV interview. He won't be too much longer, if you want to wait. Or I can give him the papers for you. I'm Haley Glen, his fiancée," she said. How strange it sounded. How disconcerting to feel a leap of pleasure over a single word.

Behind rimless glasses, the man's black crow-eyes gleamed with interest. He stepped forward and chucked the baby under the chin. "Pleased to meet you. This must be Joel Winton."

Haley stiffened instinctively, resisting the urge to pull the baby away from the man's hand. It was the first time she had heard Joel called by Sam's name. Until now, he'd been known by Ellen's surname. "Who are you?" she demanded.

The man looked flustered. "Sorry, I should have introduced myself right away. I'm Matthew McGookin, Sam's lawyer."

She didn't know why, but alarm bells went off in her head. "Is there some kind of problem?"

Matthew fumbled in the briefcase and pulled out some papers tied with thin pink cord. "Not where this little fellow's concerned. Sam's proud as punch of him. He asked me to arrange the documents giving him claim to Joel right away. After what his first wife did to him, it's no wonder he's taking no chances this time, is it?''

Claim. The word punched through Haley and she took a deep breath. *Sam didn't trust her,* she thought, amazed that a single notion had such power to wound. How could she convince him she wasn't like his ex-wife? She couldn't, Haley decided. Either Sam trusted her of his own accord, or they had nothing. ''What's this about?'' she asked.

The lawyer beamed. ''It's a statutory declaration giving him legal claim to his son.''

Claim. At the word, the floor slanted alarmingly and Haley tightened her hold on the baby. Calm. She had to keep calm. ''Sam didn't tell me he'd spoken to you.''

''He probably wants the document to be a surprise.''

She managed to nod her head. ''It's certainly that. Don't I have some say in this?''

Matthew looked surprised. ''Of course. Under your sister's will, you're the baby's legal guardian. Sam didn't need me to tell him he wouldn't stand a snow-ball's chance if you opposed his plan. So it's just as well that you're marrying him. Much better for the child if these things happen amicably.''

The truth weighed heavily on her. She had known Sam didn't love her, but to have him marry her to avoid a legal fight over Joel was too much. She had to be able to trust Sam, too, and the underhanded way he'd gone about this made it impossible There had to be another explanation.

As there was for her sister's drawings? she asked herself. She had wanted one desperately, but Sam hadn't mentioned them since she found the folder, and she—coward that she was—hadn't brought it up, either. She hadn't wanted to believe he could do such a thing. Yet he had gone to his lawyer behind her back. What else was he capable of?

Her blood chilled. Did he mean to use Joel as a bargaining chip to ensure she kept silent about the drawings? How could she bring Joel up in such an atmosphere?

She couldn't. Just as she couldn't fight Sam as long as he used the chemistry between them to manipulate her. Her response to his kisses had betrayed her. It had also nearly cost her Joel.

Her head lifted. No more. From now on she would be bulletproof where men were concerned. Man, she amended inwardly. Only one man had the power to tilt her world so far on its axis that she feared she might never right it again.

The lawyer shifted impatiently. "Then you'll give him the documents?"

She accepted them, hoping he didn't notice how badly her hand shook. "I'll give them to him." She just didn't say when.

"Thanks. I'd stick around, but I'm due in court in twenty minutes. Have Sam call me, if he has any questions."

She nodded agreement, wanting nothing so much as to tear the papers into shreds. If Matthew didn't get out of there soon, he'd be next. Luckily he was as good as his word and left, trouser legs flapping, before she could do anything she'd come to regret.

It was Sam she really wanted to attack. How dare he take steps to claim Joel without consulting her? What if he didn't mean to include her in his new family, after all? Was their engagement a ruse to keep her off guard until he completed the formalities? Once they were married, it wouldn't matter whether she stayed or not. Joel would belong to him.

His ring winked mockingly at her and she wrenched it off, flinging it onto the table. Until she knew exactly what Sam's plans were, this farce was over. She had known he didn't love her, but this was intolerable.

Chills shivered along her spine and tears of anger beaded her eyes until she dashed them away with her free hand. Joel stirred, sensing her distress. She kissed his silky cheek. "It's okay, pumpkin, I won't let anyone take you away from me."

She meant it. Sam was wealthy and influential, and also happened to be Joel's biological father, but she wouldn't rest until she had exhausted every option available to keep her baby.

She hugged him against her breast, breathing in his sweet, powdery scent. "It seems your daddy is The Beast, after all," she told him huskily. "Maybe not to you, but to me." How could she have let herself fantasize that Sam might come to love her? Her spirits plunged at the prospect of never again knowing the warmth of his arms or the power of his kiss.

Well, so be it. He had made his choice. Now it was up to her to make her own.

She gathered Joel's things and telephoned for a cab. Sam wasn't the only one with a few surprises up his sleeve.

Chapter Ten

The storm finally broke as the cab pulled up outside Miranda's town house. As Haley paid the driver, he looked at her over his shoulder. "You and your baby are going to get wet."

He couldn't get any closer to Miranda's house because it was in a cluster of similar town houses set in lush, landscaped grounds. Miranda had chosen it for its spectacular view of the lake. Now, the view was obscured by the rain sheeting across the landscape. Every time lightning spidered across the sky, Joel flinched and his small face scrunched up in terror.

"It's all right, pumpkin," Haley soothed, feeling him tremble. "Not too long until we're safe with Auntie Miranda." Right after telephoning for a cab, Haley had called her friend from Jessie's house, so she knew Miranda was at home. "I'll make a run for it," she told the driver.

She pulled off her jacket and draped it over Joel's downy head. "This will protect you. Hold tight."

By the time she reached the shelter of Miranda's front porch, Haley was shivering in the chill wind that had sprung up with the storm. When Miranda opened the front door, she gasped in dismay. "You're soaked. Come in, quickly."

Haley shook out the jacket and dropped it on the porch. "Sorry about your carpet," she said as she dripped her way inside.

Miranda took Joel from her arms and brushed the wet hair out of his eyes. His howls of fear faded to whimpers at the novelty of finding himself in new surroundings. "He's scared stiff, poor mite. Never mind the carpet. Come through and dry off before you catch your death."

Haley followed her along the hall to the bathroom where Miranda handed her a fluffy yellow bathrobe. "When you're dry, put this on. I'll take care of Joel. You're not nearly as wet as your mummy, are you, little one?"

Relieved that Joel seemed to be recovering from his fear, Haley began to peel off her sodden clothes. "I covered him with my jacket."

"While you risked pneumonia. You still haven't told me what this is all about."

Haltingly, Haley explained about Sam taking steps to claim Joel legally. "If I hadn't intercepted the papers, I still wouldn't know what Sam was planning," she finished.

Miranda gave a low whistle. "It doesn't sound like

Sam, but some men get possessive about the idea of a son.''

"He's my son. Not Sam's."

Miranda's hand stilled. "Like it or not, he *is* Sam's biological child. That has to count for something in a court of law.''

She wasn't crying, Haley told herself. Raindrops were dripping from her hair into her eyes, that was all. "Where was he when Ellen was pregnant and alone, except for me? When Joel fought his way into the world and became the center of mine?''

"It must be getting crowded in there."

Haley scrubbed her face with the towel. "What?"

"Sam seems to be in there, too."

"You're imagining things. I've left him behind for good.''

Miranda bounced Joel on her knee. "Then why does your face light up at the mention of his name? I've known him for years, and he can be self-centered and pigheaded. But I've never known him to be cruel or to lie.''

"But he stole Ellen's ideas. I've seen the proof." She had confided her discovery with Miranda during one of their long phone calls.

"The folder doesn't prove anything except that they worked together.''

"Whose side are you on, anyway?"

Busy brushing Joel's hair, Miranda smiled. "I'm on both sides, because I care about you both. Hey, don't eat that.'' Just in time, she rescued the brush before it went into the baby's mouth.

In spite of herself, Haley smiled. Then the smile faded. "He had his lawyer draw up the papers without telling me. What else can I think?"

"But asking you to marry him to keep you quiet, seems so underhanded."

And so unlike Sam, Haley read into Miranda's statement. Everything in her yearned to believe it, but too much was at stake. "I only know I had to get Joel away from him. I can't risk losing him now."

Miranda fixed her with a speculative look. "Him meaning Joel or Sam?"

"Joel, of course. Sam means nothing to me."

Miranda looked skeptical. "Whatever you say." She sneaked a glance at her watch.

Haley caught the gesture. Belatedly, she took in Miranda's stylish dress and high heels, and the careful way she'd protected her clothing with towels. "Am I keeping you from something—or someone?"

"Nothing important."

Haley didn't miss her friend's sudden reddening. "You have a date, don't you? Oh, honey, I'm sorry. I shouldn't have barged in on you like this. I'll take Joel home as soon as the storm eases."

"You'll do no such thing. I'm meeting my friend at a restaurant, and if we go anywhere, it will be back to his place, so you needn't look so worried."

"Are you sure?"

Miranda finished drying Joel and swathed him in a towel, handing him a sponge in the shape of a turtle to play with. "I'm sure about a lot of things. Yes,

you're welcome to use my place tonight because I
won't be needing it.''

Haley recalled Miranda's admission that her biological clock had started ticking right after Haley
started bringing Joel to the office. Evidently she had
taken Haley's advice to heart. Her spirits lifted for
her friend's sake. "Who's the lucky man?"

"He's the cousin of Aloys Gada I told you about.''

The one who was going to pull strings to have the
famous designer make Haley's wedding dress, Haley
remembered. Just as well she hadn't let Miranda arrange the introduction.

Masking her distress, she hugged her friend. "Have
a great time. Thanks again for letting us stay.''

Miranda looked torn. "I could stick around if you
need to talk.''

She would, too, although she was obviously looking forward to her date. Haley felt a momentary pang
of jealousy. Just because things hadn't worked out
between her and Sam, didn't mean Miranda wasn't
entitled to her shot at happiness. "Go," she insisted.
"Do just about everything I wouldn't do.''

Miranda's eyes clouded. "You will, in time.''

"Not with Sam.''

"It's a crying shame, since you're obviously crazy
about him. Last time I spoke to him, I got the impression he feels the same.''

"You're incurable.'' *And wrong,* Haley was sure.
Sam's actions weren't those of a man in love.

Miranda was silent for a moment before she said,
"I guess you know what's best for you. There's food

in the refrigerator. I don't have any baby food, but you can use the blender to puree something.''

Haley appreciated her friend dropping the subject of Sam, when Miranda obviously wanted to continue pleading his case. She was simply too tired and over-wrought to discuss it right now. Maybe tomorrow she'd be more rational. Tonight, all she wanted was to settle Joel down and fall into bed.

''Everything we need is in my bag,'' she assured Miranda. Haley didn't have a change of clothes for herself, but the borrowed robe would do until her own clothes dried. Her conscience wouldn't let her delay Miranda any longer. She all but pushed her friend toward the door.

In deference to the weather, Miranda swirled a hooded cloak around her shoulders and picked up her evening bag from the hall stand. ''Are you sure you don't want me to stay?''

She had never needed a friend more, but couldn't bring herself to spoil Miranda's night. ''You've done enough already. We'll be fine.''

The front door closed behind her and Haley let out her breath in a rush. Driven by the need to get Joel away from Sam, she hadn't given herself time to think about what to do next. She couldn't stay here. It was the first place after her own flat that he would think to look.

She busied herself settling Joel with his bottle in a cocoon of cushions on the sofa in the living room. In the kitchen she heated baby food for Joel, and scrambled some eggs for herself. Putting the food on a tray, she carried it back to the living room.

Joel fell asleep after only a few mouthfuls of food. He was tired out after the drama of the storm, poor mite. So was she, but for different reasons. Trying to think of a logical course of action was beyond her tonight. She flicked through a television guide but nothing caught her interest. She was prowling around the living room when a knock came on the front door.

Had Miranda forgotten something? She would use her key. So it had to be Sam. Haley stilled. If she was quiet, maybe he'd think no one was home and go away.

The knock startled Joel and he began to cry. She picked him up, soothing him, and he fell asleep again immediately, but it was too late. Sam must have heard the plaintive wails.

She put Joel back to bed and wrenched open the front door. Sam stood there, shaking water off a huge black umbrella. Still wearing the ivory cashmere sweater and black chinos he'd chosen for the TV interview, with raindrops beading his wide shoulders, he looked magnificent, and her throat went dry. It was too soon for this. She needed more time to erect some defenses against him. She took refuge in anger. "I hope you're satisfied. You woke the baby."

"I'll wake the whole neighborhood if you don't let me in."

"I will, but only because I don't want to cause problems for Miranda with her neighbors. How did you find us?"

"When I realized you'd gone, I pressed the redial button on Jessie's phone. The first number that came up was Miranda's. I called her and asked if she knew where you were, but she was evasive, and said she was going out. I decided to come and see her. You must have been on the way by then. When I got here, her car was gone, but all the lights were still on. Then I heard Joel crying and knew I'd found you."

Leaving the umbrella on the porch, he stepped inside and followed her into the living room. His gaze softened momentarily as he caught sight of Joel sleeping in his cocoon of pillows on the couch, but hardened again as he looked at Haley. He extended a hand, opening the fingers to reveal her engagement ring. "Would you care to explain this?"

She grabbed the legal documents she'd brought with her and slapped them into his palm, covering the ring. "When you explain this. Your lawyer brought them over for your signature. According to him, they give you legal claim to Joel." She almost spat the words out.

He didn't glance at them. "And you think I'm trying to take him away from you?"

"What else am I supposed to think?"

His mouth curled into a sneer. "You're supposed to trust me. At least that's the theory when you agree to marry someone."

"Unless it's a trick. What's the deal, Sam? I keep silent about who really created your best-selling character, or you shut me out of my baby's life?"

"With an imagination like that, you ought to be the writer, not me."

She couldn't resist it. "Maybe it runs in the family."

"You still don't get it, do you? I proposed marriage because I'm in love with you, not for any other reason."

Too stunned to respond, she began to collect the dinner things and assemble them on the tray. Why couldn't Sam have told her he loved her when he proposed? "It doesn't change anything now," she said dully.

"It should. Unless it suits you to keep a war going between us."

Her gaze flew to his face. "Why should it?"

"To keep Joel all to yourself."

"He isn't a pawn in some game between us. He's my baby."

"He's my son, too," Sam said grimly. "I thought he was going to be our son, growing up with both of us in his life. But I won't let you shut me out, so you may as well deal with reality. This is a battle you can't win."

"I'm well aware of it," she said tiredly. "I can't afford a fancy lawyer to plead my case. All I can do is show that everything I've done for Joel up to now has been out of love. It has to be enough." Her voice broke.

Sam took a half step toward her before checking himself visibly. "You'll need a stronger argument if you want to keep my son from me."

"Then try this. First his father didn't want to know about him, then I discovered proof that his father is a liar and a cheat. Not the sort of man to be given care of an innocent child." *Nor custody of her heart,* but they weren't discussing her needs. It was too late to protect herself, but not too late to save Joel from him.

Sam flinched as if she'd struck him, but he squared his shoulders. "This proof you're so certain you have doesn't amount to more than a few development sketches done by your sister."

"It's enough." *It had to be,* she told herself, wondering at the same time why Sam didn't seem troubled by her threat to expose him. Hurt by her accusations, sure, but not unduly alarmed. What was he up to?

"No, it's not." His voice cracked like the thunder outside. "It's time I set the record straight. Don't move."

He steered her to an armchair and pushed her into it, then went outside again. She debated locking him out, but didn't doubt he would break the door down if she tried. She had to think of Joel.

Sam was back in minutes with a briefcase, his hair and clothes glistening with raindrops. His face looked set and she remembered that he also disliked storms. Yet he had ventured into the full fury of one to find her. To find Joel, she reminded herself.

Sam opened the briefcase and dumped a folder of papers into her lap. She didn't look at them. "What's this?"

"Look inside."

His tone brooked no argument so she flicked through the folder listlessly, sure that nothing in it could change things between her and Sam. Until she saw what she was looking at. "When were these done?" she asked in a stunned whisper.

"When I was nineteen and first dreamed up the Cosmic Panda character. They're signed and dated, and would no doubt hold up to forensic testing if necessary."

It wasn't necessary. The dates and signatures were in the same faded pen as the drawings. All her sister had done was develop Sam's original ideas, as she had been paid to do. She mustn't have meant Haley to take her seriously when she suggested that Sam owed her some of the royalties from the books. Haley had been so caught up in her vendetta against Sam that she hadn't stopped to consider whether Ellen had been serious or not. Haley felt the color leave her face. "Oh, Sam, I'm so sorry."

He ignored the apology, and began to tick points off on his fingers. "I've answered your question about why I turned Ellen away when she told me she was pregnant. Now I've convinced you I didn't steal her ideas. What's left?"

"The legal papers."

"Ah, yes, you didn't read them, did you?"

She winced at the accusation in his tone. "I didn't have time."

"You didn't make time. If you had, you'd see that by signing them, I acknowledge I'm Joel's father and agree to take responsibility for his future needs. There's nothing there about taking him away from you. I want Joel to have two parents, not just one. You grew up without your father, so I don't have to explain to you why I consider it important.''

She shook her head. What had she done? She had accused the man she loved of every crime there was, including trying to take her baby away from her. Belatedly, it dawned on her that he had also said he had proposed marriage because he loved her. How could she have been so wrong?

She made herself meet his angry gaze. ''I've treated you shamefully, and I'm sorry, Sam. I don't know what I can do to make amends.''

''Give me my son.''

The floor dropped away beneath her. ''Anything but that.''

''Then marry me as you agreed, and we'll try to work this out like civilized adults.''

Even now, he was being fairer than she had any right to expect. It cost her everything she had to lift brimming eyes to him. She would have to let him become a full-time father to his son. It was his right. More than it was hers, if truth be admitted. Because she could never be civilized when it came to Sam. Sharing his life on any sort of platonic basis, knowing she had destroyed his love for her, would kill her.

She bowed her head. ''I won't fight you any more. Joel belongs to you. But I can't marry you.''

''Do you hate me so much?''

Her cry came from the depths of her soul. ''I don't

hate you. I love you." Couldn't he see that a marriage of convenience would never be enough, yet it was all she could expect from him now?

The documents slid from his hands and he dropped to one knee beside her chair. "What did you say?"

He didn't sound as if he was gloating, but he must be, to have driven her to confess. "I said I love you."

Instead of a look of triumph, she saw moisture glistening in his eyes. "I thought that's what you told the interviewer. If it's true, you have a hell of a way of showing it, Haley."

"It's true. I was afraid. So afraid." That he had betrayed her sister, and planned to take Joel, that he was The Beast, after all. That he would leave her as her father had done. So much fear.

He read it all in her face and pulled her into his arms. "Of me? It kills me to hear you say that when I love you so much."

"You still love me? Even after I accused you of such awful things."

He stroked her hair. "I should have explained about the drawings when you found the folder. I planned to have them framed as a surprise for you. But I was furious with you for doubting me."

"I thought it was guilt."

"I'm only guilty of one thing—loving you from the moment you walked into my life."

She gave a watery smile. "I'll never doubt you again, I promise."

"That's all I need to know." He scrambled away but it was only to retrieve the diamond ring that had dropped to the floor with the documents. A tremor racked her as he lifted her left hand and placed the ring onto her finger. It settled there like the last piece of a puzzle falling into place. "When I asked you to marry me, I was already in love with you but I didn't think you felt the same way."

"I did," she admitted. "But I was sure you only proposed for the baby's sake."

His glance went to Joel, sleeping peacefully in his nest of cushions on the sofa. "And now?"

When he looked at her with such love in his eyes, how could she possibly have any doubts? "I know you love me for myself," she said in a husky whisper. "Being parents to Joel will be wonderful, but first and foremost, we'll be lovers now and for always." The very word sent spurs of excitement leaping along her spine. "I can't bear the thought of living without you."

"Yet you were prepared to leave me."

"Only to think things through. I had no idea what I should do next."

His mouth slid across the column of her throat, tasting, teasing, the feeling so unbelievably sensuous that waves of heat ran riot through her. "I know exactly what you should do next."

He urged her down from the chair to the floor, where he gathered her into his arms. The robe fell away, exposing an expanse of creamy skin that he proceeded to lavish with kisses. She closed her eyes, feeling hot and cold by turns. But she didn't want him to stop. She didn't ever want him to stop.

His hands slid inside the robe, exploring, caressing, exciting. No one touched her the way Sam did. Her body or her heart. He touched more, she recognized. He touched a core of loneliness she hadn't known was there. Touched it, answered it, filled it. She would do the same for him, she promised herself.

"I love you so much," she said on a blissful sigh. Being able to confess her feelings felt miraculous. To know her love was returned in full measure was another miracle. "I want to keep saying it over and over."

He looked up, his eyes starry. "You won't hear any objections from me."

Her breath caught as he captured her mouth in a kiss that went on and on. Her heart shuddered with the sudden fear of too much pleasure. Then soared. What a foolish thought. Love was endless. Infinite. There was enough for baby Joel and all the children she and Sam would make together. And still all the love in the world would be left for themselves. They could never drain it dry, only increase its bounty through loving more.

"You're thinking," Sam said, the back of his hand grazing her cheek. "What about?"

She turned his hand and kissed his palm. "About us, and the future."

His fingers slid around her jaw and found her mouth. She suckled greedily and he drew a sharp, almost pained breath, as if she was testing his control to the limit. "I like the sound of that," he said in a raw voice. "But our future had better start soon, because I don't think I can wait much longer to make love to you.''

He caught her fingers and nibbled the tips. Desire speared through her. "Neither can I," she said raggedly. Was it only hours ago that the words "us" and "future" had seemed as far out of her reach as the stars he called down with his touch.

Such as *I love you.*

She said it to him again for the sheer joy of it, thrilled beyond measure to know she would be saying it—and hearing it—for all their tomorrows. For eternity. It seemed barely long enough.

Epilogue

Australia's first lady stepped to the podium. Beside her in the center of a sandstone wall was a pair of green curtains, tightly closed, a pull-cord awaiting her touch. "It's a privilege to be invited to open the first Panda Center," she said warmly. "Thanks to the generosity of Sam Winton and his family, who not only conceived the idea of a counseling center for children dealing with bereavement or separation, but who have also donated a portion of the royalties from the hugely popular Cosmic Panda books and television series. Along with the generous public response to the fundraising campaign organized by Mrs. Winton, the center will be able to help our children for many years to come. Thank you, Haley and Sam."

Haley felt a swell of pride so strong it threatened to choke her. Sam reluctantly rose to accept the applause of the invited audience. Flashlights sparkled and TV cameras whirred. He tried to pull her to her feet to share in the accolades but she resisted. This was the fruition of Sam's dream.

Early in their marriage he had told her he wanted to do more than entertain the world's children. He wanted to help them in some tangible fashion. A late-night brainstorming session between them had resulted in the idea of the Panda Center, where children who had lost a parent through separation or death could seek counseling and support face-to-face as well as by phone and on the Internet.

If Sam had his way, this wouldn't be the last such center. Watching him modestly wave away the applause of the crowd, she wondered that she could ever have thought him The Beast. He had a heart of gold, her man. And a spirit to match. When he set his heart on something, there was no stopping him.

He had set his heart on her, and look what happened, she thought, feeling a rush of pleasure at the way he had finally bulldozed through her objections, to show her how much he loved her. Even now, she loved him so intensely that it frightened her at times, until she remembered that she wasn't alone. Sam was always there for her and their children.

Joel stood by his father's side, his small hand trustingly clutched in his father's large one. At five, he was already tall for his age, and looked more like his daddy with every passing year, she thought as her heart brimmed with love for them both. He liked to mimic everything Sam did, right down to "writing" at a scaled-down computer when Sam went to his office.

When Sam found a lady-love for the Irish wolfhound, Dougal, resulting in a litter of adorable puppies, Joel had been beside himself. Just as he believed he was a miniature of his daddy, Joel was convinced the puppies were miniatures of Dougal, and had to have one for himself. He still didn't believe that the puppies would grow to the same size as their father. Like Joel himself, she thought fondly. Right now he couldn't imagine being as tall or confident as his daddy, although she could see the makings of the man he would be in the boy he was now.

Like Sam, he'd be a heartbreaker, too, one day. No, that wasn't true. Sam hadn't broken her heart. He'd come close, but he'd mended it just in time. Their daughter was proof of their love.

Haley's eyes strayed to Ellie, perched on the edge of a seat alongside her, her chubby legs dangling. She was bored, poor love. "It won't be long now," she whispered.

"Then can I have some cake?"

"As soon as the speeches are finished," Haley said. "We have to listen now. The governor-general's wife is about to open the Panda Center."

"It's already open," Ellie insisted. "Look."

"It's a pretend opening, so they can take pictures of the first lady with your daddy."

Ellie screwed up her face. "Don't want daddy in a picture with that lady. I want him in a picture with you."

"He will be soon," Haley assured her, checking to be sure her camera was handy. "You can be in a picture, too, if you want."

Ellie nodded vigorously, kicking her legs. "Yes, please. Will the new baby be in a picture, too?"

"We already have a picture of him," Haley said, thinking of the blurry ultrasound photograph tucked in her album at home. She and Sam had seen enough to know their baby would be a boy. Ellie had already decided to name him Dougal, although they'd have to talk about that. Single-minded, these children of hers, Haley thought fondly. "He's way too little to be in a proper photograph yet," she assured her daughter.

"How long?"

Haley counted months. "At least until Christmas."

Ellie's face brightened. "Is Santa Claus bringing the new baby?"

"No, darling." She dropped an arm around her daughter's thin shoulders. "Tell you what, why don't you ask your daddy to explain it to you after we get home. He's the storyteller in the family."

He'd love that, she thought as her spirits soared. She looked forward to hearing Sam explain the facts of life to a three-year-old. For someone whose stock-in-trade was words, he could be robbed of them amazingly easily by his little daughter.

He wasn't the only one, she thought happily, filled with pride as the other guests crowded around her husband. He stood a head taller than most of the group, and she didn't miss the flirtatious way some of the women looked at him. She wasn't jealous, seeing the looks as evidence of her good taste. Being married to him still felt like a kind of miracle, and it frequently left her speechless. Just as well they had other means of communication at their disposal.

She lifted Ellie off the seat and picked up the camera. "Let's go join your daddy and Joel."

He saw them coming and held out his hand. She slipped hers into it, feeling the same sense of excitement and arousal that she always did the moment he touched her. She could hardly wait until they were alone.

It wouldn't be for some time, she realized as she heard Ellie's piping voice. "Daddy, Mommy said you'd tell me..."

On Ellie went, blurting out her question about who delivered babies, heedless of the bemused looks her question generated among the distinguished guests. Sam's wry grin reached Haley over the child's head. "Oh, did she now. Well, Mommy's going to have some explaining of her own to do when we get home."

His gaze was so warm and his voice so redolent with promise that she could hardly wait.

*   *   *   *   *

Don't miss Valerie Parv's
next Silhouette Romance,
CODE NAME: PRINCE,

part of the newest installment of
the popular miniseries
ROYALLY WED,
on sale May 2001!

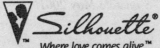

MAITLAND MATERNITY

Where the luckiest babies are born!

In March 2001, look for

BILLION DOLLAR BRIDE
by Muriel Jensen

Billionaire Austin Cahill doesn't believe in love or marriage—

he only wants to marry in order to produce an heir. Single mom and wedding planner Anna Maitland is horrified by his old-fashioned attitude. So when Austin proposes a marriage of convenience, will Anna be able to refuse him... now that she's fallen in love with him?

Each book tells a different story about the world-renowned Maitland Maternity Clinic— where romances are born, secrets are revealed... and bundles of joy are delivered.

HARLEQUIN®
Makes any time special ™

Silhouette®
Where love comes alive ™

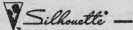

International Bestselling Author

DIANA PALMER

At eighteen, Amanda Carson left
west Texas, family scandal and a man
she was determined to forget. But the Whitehall
empire was vast, and when the powerful family wanted
something, they got it. Now they wanted Amanda—and her
advertising agency. Jace Whitehall, a man Amanda hated and
desired equally, was waiting to finish what began years ago.
Now they must confront searing truths about both their
families. And the very thing that drove Amanda from this
land might be the only thing able to keep her there.

THE *Cowboy* AND THE *Lady*

"Nobody tops Diana Palmer."
—Jayne Ann Krentz

Available February 2001 wherever paperbacks are sold!